A Dope Boy's Queen

Lock Down Publications and
Ca$h Presents
A Dope Boy's Queen
A Novel by Aryanna

Lock Down Publications

P.O. Box 944
Stockbridge, Ga 30281

Visit our website
www.lockdownpublications.com

Copyright 2020 by Aryanna
A Dope Boy's Queen

First Edition June 2020
Printed in the United States of America

Lock Down Publications
Like our page on Facebook: Lock Down Publications @
www.facebook.com/lockdownpublications.ldp
Cover design and layout by: **Dynasty Cover Me**
Book interior design by: **Shawn Walker**
Edited by**: Kiera Northington**

Stay Connected with Us!

Text **LOCKDOWN** to 22828 to stay up-to-date
with new releases, sneak peeks, contests and more…

Submission Guideline.

Submit the first three chapters of your completed manuscript to ldpsubmissions@gmail.com, subject line: Your book's title. The manuscript must be in a .doc file and sent as an attachment. The document should be in Times New Roman, double-spaced and in size 12 font. Also, provide your synopsis and full contact information. If sending multiple submissions, they must each be in a separate email.

Have a story but no way to send it electronically? You can still submit to LDP/Ca$h Presents. Send in the first three chapters, written or typed, of your completed manuscript to:

LDP: Submissions Dept
P.O. Box 944
Stockbridge, Ga 30281

DO NOT send original manuscript. Must be a duplicate.

Provide your synopsis and a cover letter containing your full contact information.

Thanks for considering LDP and Ca$h Presents.

Dedication

This book is dedicated to the absolute love of my life. Clyde ain't shit without Bonnie! Big Fact$!

Acknowledgements

All glory to God, the Most High, all knowing and all seeing. Without you, I'm less than nothing. I have to thank the one person who completes me and gives me my strength to face the hardships. Good times are only good because of you and bad times don't faze me because you're there, too. You're my true best friend and I love you, baby! It took us a LONG TIME to get back to where we should be but I'll never let you go again. Kirsten J., MY BONNIE, MY MIKKO', you are THE BADDEST BITCH EVER!!!!! I have to thank the original diva squad, Mariah J., Sharday J., and my namesake, Aryanna. I love you like I never left and nothing and no one in this world can or will change that. To the addition to the squad, Jordyn (J baby), you're in my heart too and I want you to always know that. I have to thank my fans, my fans, MY F-A-N-S! You made me and you make me humble. Thank you and I love you. I have to thank my family (the ones I fuck with). I love you all for loving me. Blood makes us related but loyalty makes us family. Remember that! I have to thank my LDP FAMILY for continuing to push me in the right direction. Your success motivates me. I have to thank ALL MY HATERS!! Heyyyyyy! Lol! Alright let's do this roll call: Polo, what up, my dude? Take the Hype Program to new heights! Baby D, what's really good? P-TOWN STAND UP! Juan Lee, I love you, son. Lol! Ayo Marc, meal on you! Rex, I love you, cuzzo I'll see you soon. Chubbs, it's ALL APE SHIT!! Red Gunz, your wisdom still rings in my ear. Moreno, what's shakin' with you? Ashley, I fucks with you, slim, and shoutout to your godchildren. To the niggas I fuck with at Haynesville Correctional Center, don't let the pandemic break your spirit. If it ain't life it ain't long! What up, Boyd? I see you Coleman and to the rest of the dudes and females incarcerated world wide, I GOTCHU and I'm gonna put on for you!!! LDP, THE GAME IS OURS!

Aryanna

Chapter 1

Carol City, FL
December 2023

"Were the terms of our agreement unclear in any way?" I asked, calmly.

N-no, Claudette, but—"

"Were the terms of our agreement *unfair* in any way?" I asked.

"They w-were more than fair. Claudette, please, I—"

"So, then why, Domonique? Why would you not have my money on time?" I asked, looking down into his badly beaten face.

"I'll get your money! I'll get your money, I swear, just please don't hurt them," he begged, sobbing uncontrollably.

The "them" he was referring to was his trophy wife strapped to the chair next to him, and their two young sons, who were tied up in the corner of the office we were currently occupying. Truthfully, they had nothing to do with my business arrangement with Domonique, but the graveyard was full of people who were there as a result of being collateral damage. Guilt by association was a very real thing.

"Domonique, where's my money?" I asked.

"I can have it to you in forty-eight hours, I swear. I just…"

"Well, if you don't have my money then *surely* you have my product," I stated reasonably.

"Claudette, *please*, I've always paid you before—"

"And you'll pay now too. One way or the other," I said, moving away from him so Tony could get back to work.

In appearance alone, Tony's dark-skinned, six-five, three-hundred-forty-pound frame was enough to inspire cooperation from most people, not to mention the low, gravelly whisper he spoke in. If he actually had to put his hands on you though, you'd know *real* fear and unspeakable pain. Domonique was now one of many who could attest to that, *if* dead men told stories. While Tony went back to making a mess of Domonique's face, I decided to switch tactics.

"Denise, I think it's time we have a woman-to-woman conversation," I said, pulling up a chair next to the clearly frightened and trembling white woman, whose only mistake was marrying a nothing ass nigga.

"I-I don't know any-anything," Denise stammered.

"Well, I wouldn't say that you don't know *any*thing. I'm pretty sure you're smart enough to know the house you live in, the cars you drive, the vacations you take, and the private school your kids go to isn't all paid for by this restaurant we're sitting in. I'm sure business is good, but not *that* good. So, I think you know about your husband's extracurricular activities, but if not, I'm willing to enlighten you since we have time. Your husband sells drugs, large quantities of cocaine to be specific, and I'm his supplier. Now, I gave him a half-ton of almost pure cocaine, but I still haven't received payment for it. Do you understand the problem with that?"

"Y-yes, but that had nothing to do with me or my k-kids. We shouldn't be here," she replied emotionally.

"Well, that's not completely accurate. Domonique spends money on you and those kids, *my money*, which technically means you all belong to me. See how that works?" I asked.

Denise had already been crying, but my words reduced her to a sobbing that sounded like nails on a chalkboard. There was no way I was about to sit here and listen to this shit for hours!

"Hold up a minute, Tony," I said, getting up and walking out of the office and into the huge kitchen.

With it being the middle of the night, there was nobody in the entire building except for the office, so I had to hunt for what I was looking for. It took me a few minutes to find it but once I did, I headed straight back to the office.

"Okay, Domonique, it's time to find out what you love more," I said, waving the meat cleaver in front of the one eye he could still see out of.

"Please, Claudette," he mumbled through swollen lips.

"Begging doesn't make my money or product appear. Now, I would start with your bitch, but I know you've got at least two mistresses, so Denise don't mean all that much to you. Tony, bring one of the kids over to the desk and lay his hand on the top of it, palm down," I instructed.

"No! Please, no!" Denise screamed, trying in vain to break free of the zip ties that had her bound to the metal chair she was sitting in.

I ignored her and Domonique's pleas, because I was fed up with all the bullshit. Instead, I calmly went to the desk, raised the meat cleaver high above my head, and separated the boy's hand from his wrist with one blow. I was positive everyone's screams could be heard throughout the entire restaurant, but it didn't matter to me because I only had one goal in mind. Getting my money. I picked up the little boy's hand and walked back over to Domonique.

"I'm not sure how long you've got before your little guy bleeds to death, but you might want to hurry. So, where's-my-money?" I asked, tapping him on the head with his son's bloody hand.

"In my account offshore, but there's only a million! You can have it and I'll get you the rest, I *swear*!" Domonique replied, clearly fighting hysteria.

"Give me your account information," I said, dropping the hand and pulling out my phone.

In less than ten minutes, I had the money transferred into my account, but now I was pissed off that this motherfucker had actually made me go through all that.

"You know, Domonique, you're a real piece of shit. All of this could've been avoided, but you're greedy and you think because I got a pussy, it makes me one. Look at the scars on my face. Do I look pussy to you?" I asked, getting close to him so he could see my battle wounds up close.

"I'm s-sorry, Claudette, I really am. Please just let my family go," he pleaded.

"You want me to let them go? Okay. Tony gather everyone around Domonique real quick," I said, taking a step back.

The little boy now missing his hand had lost consciousness, so Tony carried him over and laid him at Domonique's feet. He did the same thing with Domonique's other son, despite his squirming and struggling against the zip ties holding his hands and feet together.

"Say goodbye to everyone, Domonique," I ordered.

"Denise, I-I love you and—"

His speech was interrupted by the deafening roar of the two-tone chrome .45 coming to life in my hand.

"Don't look at me like that because you know damn well you didn't love that bitch. Now, say goodbye to your sons," I instructed.

"Claudette, *please*, they're kids for God's sake! They're only ten and eleven years old, you *can't* kill them," Domonique begged hysterically.

I'd never seen this side of him before. Domonique wasn't a weak nigga, he actually commanded respect in the street as well as fear, but I couldn't see any of that in the man in front of me. Experience had thought me that anyone could be broken, but the way Domonique had played his hand had led me to believe he wouldn't fold this quick. Obviously, I was wrong. Without a word, I took aim at one boy and put a gaping hole in his head, before turning the gun on the other one and doing the same thing. I'd expected Domonique to scream until his lungs exploded, but instead, he got a faraway look in his eyes.

"No need to be shocked, my nigga, I did them both a favor. They probably would've turned out like you and that would've just been a disappointment, because you *definitely* ain't built for this," I said sincerely.

"Just kill me," Domonique mumbled.

"You read my mind," I replied, raising my pistol and putting a bullet through his remaining good eye.

"I'm hungry, Tony, what about you?" I asked, looking at my right-hand man.

"I could eat."

"Good. Burn this bitch to the ground and let's go," I said, tucking my pistol back into the waist of my red linen suit.

"Right away, Mrs. Snow."

Aryanna

Chapter 2

5 years earlier

"Honey, I'm home!"

"I'm in the kitchen, babe," I replied, grabbing the potholders off the counter so I could remove my pot roast from the oven.

"*Damn,* it smells good in here," Zion said, coming into the kitchen, carrying a dozen, long stem red roses.

"Of course, it does. You know I can burn," I replied smiling.

"Mmm, yes you can, but who said I was talking about the food?" he said, moving swiftly up behind me and kissing my neck gently.

I had to concentrate hard to sit the pot roast on top of the stove because Zion's presence alone tended to fuck with my senses and motor skills. Even after five years of marriage, the butterflies in my stomach were as lively as the first time I'd seen the six foot one, two-hundred-twenty-pound, coffee-complexioned god of a man now walking his lips along my collarbone right now. He'd been the starting point guard for a rival varsity high school basketball team, but I hadn't been able to focus on his game because his looks had me wishing I'd invested in waterproof panties. That night, I'd done something completely out of character for me. I stepped to him and asked for his number. My boldness intrigued him, especially since I still made him work to get the pussy. He did put in that work though and six years later, he was *still* putting that work in.

"So, are we gonna eat dinner, or skip straight to dessert?" I asked teasingly.

"You *know* what I wanna do, but I do have a last-minute business appointment," he replied, taking a step back.

"Ah, so this explains the flowers," I said, turning around and crossing my arms over my chest, while staring up into his dark brown eyes.

The smile he gave me was sheepish and apologetic, but it didn't stop the anger and disappoint flowing through my body. It was on the tip of my tongue to say some real foul shit, like, *I was too sexy to be sitting at home alone, playing with my pussy, so maybe I should find a side piece.* The consequence behind that statement wasn't the action I was looking for tonight though. Despite me being five foot four, and a hundred and fifty-seven pounds of gravity defying curves, I could handle my own against anybody, but a fight with Zion wasn't what I really wanted.

"You're working late…again?" I asked slowly, fighting to contain my frustration.

"I know this is supposed to be our date night, but something completely unexpected came up. I'm sorry, sweetheart."

I was on the verge of believing his sincerity but when I looked down at the hands now extending the red roses towards me, I noticed something.

"Something unexpected came up, huh? Does it have anything to do with the blood under your fingernails?" I asked, looking at him hard.

He glanced briefly at his hands, before putting the flowers on the counter and moving to the sink to wash his hands. While he did that, I turned my attention back to my dinner plans, carrying the pot roast into the dining room. The table was already set, the red wine was chilling on ice, and despite Zion having other plans, I wasn't about to let my hard work go to waste. I made myself a plate of the succulent meat, accompanied by the baby potatoes and mixed vegetables cooked in the roast's juices, and I took my seat.

"You know you're sexy when you're angry, right?" he asked, from the dining room doorway.

I ignored his question and began eating, determined not to let my mood be ruined any further tonight. I could feel his eyes staring a hole through me, but I continued right on enjoying my food. I expected him to leave me alone so he could go handle whatever he had to handle, instead he surprised me by coming over and pouring me a glass of wine. My surprise turned to shock when he actually fixed himself a plate of food and sat down across from me.

"Zion, look, if you need—"

"So, how was class today, did you learn anything new?" he asked, pouring himself a glass of wine.

"You know damn well you don't wanna talk about my law school class, so why you fakin?"

"I think we both know I have vested interest in you obtaining your law degree, babe," he replied, smirking.

Sometimes he infuriated me *so bad*, but somehow, he always managed to turn it around and have me smiling sooner than I wanted to be. Just like right now.

"Yeah, well that's because you keep doing dumb shit to get blood on your hands. Literally. Now tell me what happened," I demanded.

"Tell me about your day first," he countered.

I tried to stare him down and make him bend to my will, but we both knew it wasn't gonna work.

"I'm thinking about actually attending class in person instead of doing the online thing," I said.

"And who's gonna watch Junior?"

"The nanny can—"

"Nah, the nanny *can't* because I told you from the jump my son wouldn't be raised by the help. We not 'bout to have no bougie ass kid that gets eaten alive by the real world," he said, shaking his head vigorously.

We'd had this argument enough pertaining to Zion Junior, but I didn't understand how Zion couldn't understand the challenge of attending law school *and* raising a three-year-old. A *spoiled* three-year-old!

"Zion it's no different than the nanny being here during the day to help me with Junior," I replied.

"It *is* different because you're still here to teach him, interact with him, and beat his little ass when necessary."

"You know it's against the law to spank kids now, so—"

"And I know you're black, so you ain't hearing that shit any more than I am. We got our asses whooped growing up, and look how we turned out," he said.

"Is it too soon to point out the fact that you *just* washed the blood off of your hands?" I asked, sarcastically.

He quickly stuck his tongue out at me, causing me to laugh, despite the seriousness of the conversation.

"Look, man, I know you and you ain't worried about our son turning soft. You worried about dudes trying to hit on me if I'm out there moving and shaking in the world," I said, seriously.

"Why would I be worried about that? I mean, you're a beautiful redbone with a gorgeous smile, stunning face, and banging body, *plus* you're intelligent. Baby, you *lit* so why wouldn't a dude try to holla, even a gay mufucka would holla," he replied, chuckling.

"Oh, and you're okay with that all of a sudden?"

"Sure, I am because I know who *I am*, and I know you know who I am too. Is it too soon for me to point out the fact that I just washed the blood off my hands?" he replied, smiling devilishly before putting a piece of pot roast in his mouth.

All I could do was shake my head because I know there was no point in entertaining or continuing this portion of the conversation.

"So, you want me cooped up in the house with our son as my only company?" I asked.

"No, sweetheart, and I'm sorry I haven't been around much lately. It's taken more of my time and attention to get this restaurant off the ground, especially since I only just inherited it and didn't build it from the ground up."

"Inherited it? I like how you put that, it's nicer than saying you muscled a mufucka out of his business," I said.

"That's because I *didn't* muscle him, babe. He owed a debt, he couldn't pay, and the restaurant was the only thing he had of value. It was a win-win, because now I've got a legitimate way of justifying the income that comes from my extracurricular activities."

"Speaking of extracurricular, what happened tonight?" I asked again.

"Are you asking as my wife or as my future attorney?" he retorted.

"Both, nigga, now stop stalling and tell me what the fuck you got us into."

Despite my aggressive tone, Zion smiled, and I knew it was because he understood he had a ryder in me. He was born and raised in Florida and I came from a Louisiana parish, but we both came from the mud, and we understood that *nobody's* hands were ever completely clean. Zion had that *don't give a fuck* attitude when it came to the streets and its politics, whereas I had the mentality of there being a right way to do the wrong thing. I agreed with Zion that my place wasn't on the front line beside him, but I was still an ear he knew he could trust.

"My last shipment was almost jacked, and I found out today who was behind that failed mission," Zion said nonchalantly.

"I'm assuming you took care of him, so..."

"So just because you take care of an individual, don't mean you're taken care of the problem. When there's a situation, you gotta treat it like you're in the Ukraine and kill everything, down to the sheep dog," he replied seriously.

In no way was I an expert on the guerrilla tactics used to maintain a street empire, so in situations like this I simply absorbed what Zion said. They were jewels and I knew the value of a precious stone.

"Well, it sounds like you have business to handle, so I will accept a rain check for tonight's date night," I said.

"I appreciate that, baby, but I'm not about to leave all this good food for you to eat by yourself. I respect the effort you put into us having some grown and sexy time, and by the way, that dress *definitely* makes it clear what's for dessert," he replied, looking at me with a different hunger in his eyes.

I felt myself blushing and as our eye contact remained steady, I could feel my pussy throbbing against my thong's satin fabric.

"I was hoping you'd like the dress, especially because I knew you'd flip about the five-thousand-dollar price tag that came with it," I said.

"I love the dress, and that copper color brings out the beauty of your skin. The price don't matter, you look so good you could've bought *two* dresses and I wouldn't have cared."

"I doubt that," I replied laughing.

Suddenly, the look in his eyes changed to one I'd seen before, and I knew he somehow felt like I'd challenged him.

Slowly, he rose to his feet and extended his hand to me. I hesitated for half a second, but once I put my silverware down, I put my hand in his and he pulled me to my feet.

"Do you trust me?" he asked.

"What type of question is that?"

"Do you trust me?" he asked again, pulling me right up against his chest.

"Of course I do, bae. I trust you more than anyone in the world," I replied genuinely.

He kissed me once softly on my lips before taking a tiny step back. When he grabbed the front of my dress, I thought he intended to pull my breasts free from the clinging leather material, but then I caught sight of the pearl-handle straight razor he always carried.

"B-bae, what are you—"

"If you trust me, then don't ask questions," he said, smiling mischievously.

My mouth remained open, but I didn't utter a word as he brought the razor in his right hand to the top of my strapless dress, directly in between my titties. I could feel my heart beating faster, but it was in sync with the steady hammering happening in between my thighs, and I wasn't mad at that. In my mind, I thought he was doing all of this jokingly, but then his hand started to move slowly downward, slicing through the leather like warm butter. Within seconds, my five-thousand-dollar Gucci dress became a five-thousand-dollar bath robe, but it was evident Zion didn't care, because his attention was now on my 38-D cups.

"You're absolutely gorgeous," he whispered, grabbing ahold of my thong and cutting it off my body just as quickly.

"I'm glad you think so after all this time, and I hope you still think so when I'm old and wrinkled."

"Baby, it don't matter if you're twenty-four or eighty-four, you'll always be the most gorgeous woman in the world, and the woman I crave more than anything," he replied genuinely, staring deeply into my eyes with love's passion clouding his vision.

"Prove it," I whispered seductively.

Suddenly, the razor vanished, and my plate went crashing to the floor as I was lifted onto the table and put in its place. His lips found mine, and our kiss matched the hunger I'd seen swim to the surface in his eyes as soon as I'd spoken my challenge. I could feel him fumbling with his belt, while our tongues danced under the opening bell of this twelve-round heavyweight fight, and my own hunger made me reach down to assist. I wasted no time pulling his dick out and he wasted even less time diving inside me.

"Yes, baby!" I moaned, immediately locking my legs around him and holding on tight.

Not for a moment did he act like he had any intention of being gentle with me, but I *loved* it. Each stroke was having the effect of turning the handle on a sink, causing the pressure to build and my pussy juices to flow faster. I could feel his dick throbbing inside me already, beating against my pussy walls like a drum line and making the sweetest music of my life.

"I-I love you! I love you, Zion!" I yelled passionately.

"You too, bae, I love y-you too," he growled, fucking me harder.

Right about now I was thankful the nanny had taken our son to get ice cream, because with this pipe my man was laying, there was *no way* to remain quiet. Somehow, I managed to get his shirt over his head and off because I needed to feel the heat of his skin on my own. Two minutes later, my world was ripped apart by my first orgasm, forcing me to chant

Zion's name like I was a groupie at a concert. I knew by the trembling in his body he wasn't far behind me, but suddenly he changed speeds, and the strokes he delivered became those long, slow, thorough explorations that made it harder for me to breathe.

"Mmm, b-bae, don't tease me," I begged, knowing he could keep up this particular onslaught until I was reduced to tears of joy.

"Shhh, just take it," he instructed.

More dishes went flying off the table as he cleared room to lay me flat on my back, but the meal was the farthest thing from my mind. Zion quickly made it clear he was still hungry though, because no sooner had my back hit the table, than he replaced his dick with his tongue. The way he sucked my clit had me knocking shit off the table as I searched blindly for something, *anything*, to hold onto. When he pushed a finger deep inside my hot pussy while rapidly flicking his tongue back and forth across my clit, I lost all control and grabbed his head tightly. The beautiful torture lasted for five minutes, but that was long enough to make me cum so hard, I could feel myself squirting all over Zion's face. I could tell he didn't give a fuck though, because he slurped and savored every drop, before standing back up and shoving his dick back inside me. The aftershocks he set off were *real*, and the way he was pounding me had my eyes flickering like I was taking pictures of my brain.

"Ziiiiii-on!" I sang out, instantly feeling the fire inside me get better.

"I love you, b-baby!" he declared passionately.

I could feel his love in every backbreaking blow that caused my nerve endings to scream, and by the time we came together, I was sure he knew how much I loved him. My body felt like warm Jello and I couldn't move off the dining room table if I wanted to.

"I d-don't know how you're still-still standing," I said breathlessly, looking up at his lazy grinning face.

"My pride won't let me collapse, but you know I want to," he replied, reluctantly pulling his dick out of me and slumping in the chair behind him.

It took me a few minutes to sit up, but when I finally did, the destruction we'd caused was shocking.

"Damn, bae, for real?" I asked, looking around at the broken dishes, ruined food, and spilled wine covering the wood floor.

"Uh, I guess that's my bad, huh?" he replied, smiling unapologetically.

"You damn right, Negro! You fucked up a perfectly good dinner with your—"

"With my perfectly good dick," he concluded, winking at me.

I wanted to say something smart, but I felt the smile lighting up my face, so it was pointless denying the truth.

"I guess good dick is worth some broken dishes," I conceded, climbing down off the table.

"I'm glad we agree," he said, smacking me on the ass.

"Did you have to ruin my dress though?"

"It's okay, you can go buy another one tomorrow. Fuck it, get two," he replied, grabbing his shirt off the ground and putting it back on.

"Uh, hold up, I *know* you don't think you're about to leave me here to clean this shit up by myself," I said.

"Baby, you know I've got business to handle, and I'm already running late."

I wanted to argue, but I knew it was pointless. Plus, I never wanted to fight and be the distraction he didn't need when he had serious business to handle.

"You owe me," I said, pulling him towards me for a kiss.

"I got you, bae, I'll even wake you up with the dick when I come in."

"You promise?" I asked seductively.

"On my soul."

Aryanna

Chapter 3

I was snatched from my sleep feeling disoriented, sitting straight up in my bed, staring blindly into the endless shadows. I knew I'd been dreaming, and even though I couldn't remember exactly what the dream was about, I knew it hadn't been a bad one. That made the irrational beating of my heart in my chest even harder to explain. Something woke me up, but I didn't know what it was, until I heard the loud pounding again. I reached to my right to nudge Zion awake, but all I felt was cold silk beneath my fingertips, signifying I was alone in bed. I didn't know where my husband was, but I did know I had to go answer the front door before whoever it was woke my son up. When I grabbed the black Taurus .25 pistol out of my bedside drawer, it wasn't because I was afraid, it was because I was pissed and determined to shoot a motherfucker if this late-night visit wasn't an emergency. After pulling on one of Zion's t-shirts to cover my nakedness, I quickly made my way downstairs, turning on lights as I went. By the time I'd reached the bottom of the stairs, the instant pounding had started again.

"Who the fuck is it?" I yelled, flipping the safety off my gun as I approached the door.

"Police."

That one word forced me to flip the safety back on just as fast, right before I dropped the gun into the umbrella stand by the door. I took a deep breath and prepared my mind for mental warfare.

"What do you want?" I asked curtly, opening the door only wide enough for me to be seen. I knew it was in a cop's nature to be nosy, and allegedly seeing shit in plain sight was how they got around having a valid search warrant to run in people's houses. I knew Zion didn't keep shit in the house, but I still didn't want the cops in my spot.

Ma'am, are you Mrs. Claudette Snow?" a short, white cop in a standard Dade County police uniform asked.

"I am," I replied.

"Ma'am, we'd like to speak with you for a moment, is it possible for us to come in?" he asked, gesturing towards his silent partner.

"Do you have a warrant?" I asked, looking back and forth between the two to see which one would produce the necessary paperwork.

"No, ma'am, we don't have a warrant, but—"

"If you don't have a warrant, then you ain't coming in," I stated plainly.

"Ma'am, we just want to talk—"

"My husband has a lawyer if you wanna talk, so if there's nothing else, I'm going back to bed and you can—"

"Your husband is dead. This was a courtesy call, but since you wanna be an asshole, we'll just tell you out here," the taller, quiet cop blurted out.

I don't know why, but my eyes immediately went to those of the first cop who'd spoken to me, hoping I'd see a different truth on his face. I didn't though. I saw the tiniest bit of compassion, but it was clear that no lies were being told at this time of night.

"We'll let you get back to your beauty sleep now," the rude cop said, turning and walking away.

"I'm sorry," his partner whispered, before following his lead.

Despite the muggy night air swirling around me, I felt a chill that went bone deep. I could faintly hear the sounds of the lively insects and creatures in the distance, but the loudest thing was the screaming in my brain that was growing steadily louder. Zion *couldn't* be dead. He just couldn't be! The sight of the cops' car moving off into the night forced me to close the door on the outside world, but denial had me locked in a world of my own. I made no conscious effort to sit, yet somehow, I ended up with my back pressed to the front door and my legs stretched out in front of me. After a while, the screaming in my head stopped and the logical side of me accepted that the police had simply made a mistake. It may have been someone who *looked* like Zion or someone who was known to be *around* Zion, but it wasn't actually him. My husband wasn't dead. He was only twenty-five years old, with his entire life in front of him, so there was no way that he could be dead. There was no way I was a widow at twenty-four and my three-year-old would never know his father the way I did. All of these things were *impossible*! Part of me wanted to get up, call Zion, and tell him to bring his black ass home so all of this would be cleared up, but something kept me seated. Something kept me rooted to that spot where reality was what I said it was, because if I got up and Zion didn't answer…or if Zion didn't come home…then what? No matter how much had happened in the streets, or how ugly our fights got, I still never imagined my life without Zion in it. Never. How did I do that now? What would it look like? I couldn't answer those questions, any more than I could accept what the cops said, so all I could do was sit still and wait. I had no idea what exactly I was waiting for. If it was a sign from God, or grief to overtake me, I didn't know, but I sat in the same spot and waited. I had no idea how long it had been, but a sudden knock at my back jarred me from my semi-catatonic state. When I rose slowly to my feet, I noticed the current orange light all around me, announcing the rising sun outside and the beginning of a new day.

"It was a dream. It was all a terrible dream," I whispered to myself, knowing as soon as I opened the door, I'd find my husband on the other side. I quickly jerked the door open, but the face waiting on the other side wasn't the one I wanted to see. In fact, the man standing there finally allowed the truth I'd been fighting against, to invade my mind in a way that was inescapable.

"T-Tony, what are you doing here?" I asked, unable to make eye contact with the deadly, yet gentle giant staring at me.

"I came to check on you, Claudette. I came to make sure that you and Junior were okay."

"Tony…is-is it true? Is Zion really gone?" I asked softly, hating the way the question tasted leaving my mouth.

Tony was part of the crew Zion did business with, but him and Zion had become fast friends, years before that. There was something about murder that certain types could bond over, and Big Tony definitely had blood on his hands. Like Zion though, he had two sides to his personality, and he could be caring when he wanted to be. Tony didn't respond to the question I asked. Instead, he opened his arms and allowed me to step into his embrace. The moment my face hit his chest, I lost the battle my denial had been waging with my grief and I sobbed. I sobbed in a way I never had before, because I knew there could be no more happiness in my world now. I hadn't simply lost my husband and the father to my child. I'd lost my *soulmate*. I'd lost myself. And so, I cried. I cried for all the years we'd never have together, for all the love we'd never make, and for all the time we'd wasted. I cried for my son and the lifetime of pain he would know now. Most of all though, I cried because life was so damn unfair, and I didn't deserve for my love story to end like this. Most women might've been embarrassed to come unglued like that in front of an acquaintance, but I didn't care, and Tony didn't judge. It took me a long time to finally regain control, but Tony didn't rush me in the slightest.

"Wh-what happened?" I asked, taking a step back.

"Maybe we should talk inside," he suggested.

I hadn't realized we were still standing in the doorway, or that I was only wearing a t-shirt. Zion's t-shirt.

"Come in, I'm sorry. I'll be right back," I said, showing him to the living room before going upstairs.

My intention was to pull myself together and put some clothes on, but somehow, I ended up outside my son's door watching him sleep. I could feel the tears sliding soundlessly down my face with every rise and fall of his little chest, and the ache that accompanied them was too powerful for words. How was I gonna tell this innocent little boy that his hero, the man he loved most in the world, was gone? How did I make that alright for him? I didn't know, and I doubted if the answers to the millions of questions I had would manifest anytime soon. With my heart still shattering in my chest, I moved away from my son's door, and forced myself to enter my own room. Zion's energy was everywhere around me, but instead of allowing that to add to my grief, I used it as motivation. I had no doubt Zion would want me to be strong in the face of this devastation, and I knew it would only get worse before it got better. I just had to keep pushing. I blindly threw on some shorts and put a bra on, but I kept Zions's black t-shirt on. When I got back downstairs, I found Tony sitting on the couch wearing a blank expression on his face. I started to sit next to him but doing that would've given me a clear view of the dining room, and the memories of last night. I wasn't ready for that yet, so I sat in the overstuffed chair across from him.

"What happened, Tony?" I asked.

"Somebody got the drop on him and shot him twice."

"Who?" I asked.

"There was a situation he was looking into and—"

"I know about the botched robbery, but Zion told me he'd already taken care of the nigga responsible," I interjected.

I could tell by the look on Tony's face that he was surprised to learn Zion and I had few secrets.

"Yeah, he did take care of the nigga responsible, but it was dude's second-in-command who…who got to Zion," Tony replied.

I took a second to process what I'd just heard, fighting the endless wave of tears inside me, while trying to figure out what the fuck I was gonna do next.

"So, since you know who did it, are your people gonna handle it?" I asked.

"Actually, that's part of the reason I'm here too. My boss wants to express his condolences in person and talk to you about what happens next."

"I've never met whoever it is you work for. I mean, Zion didn't really keep shit from me, but I didn't ask questions that didn't need asking. I need to ask you though, is your boss someone I can trust?" I asked, searching his face intently for the truth.

"You can't trust anyone, Claudette, you know that."

"You're right, I do know that, but I needed to know you'd keep shit one hundred with me. Let me call someone to watch Junior, and then we can go," I replied, standing up and heading back upstairs to make the necessary phone call.

I wasn't sure how I should feel about this unexpected meeting, but I know I needed to look someone in the eye and know my husband didn't die in vain. I needed to know he would be avenged. Within an hour, I'd managed to take a shower, dress to impress, and get Junior's nanny Rosalinda to come to the house to stay with him. I didn't ask Tony where we were going as I slid in the passenger seat of his blood-red 2018 Ferrari Spyder, but surprisingly, I wasn't anxious at all.

I was numb. A quick half-hour later, we were cruising through a Miami suburb lined with multimillion-dollar homes, but I didn't know this was our destination until Tony stopped at a gated house.

"Who lives here?" I asked, looking around at the armed security walking along the grounds.

"His name is Campa, and he comes from old money. Cartel drug money to be exact. All you need to know and remember is that he's ruthless, and nothing is *ever* free when it comes to him. Nothing," Tony replied adamantly, looking me squarely in the eyes.

We quickly passed through security and once we got up to the house, we were led around to the back patio by a maid. Sitting at a table, next to an infinity pool was a slightly built Spanish man, wearing a white linen suit and no shoes. His long hair was pulled into a tight ponytail, and sunglasses covered his eyes, despite the sun barely being in the sky. It looked like his attention was fully captured by the lobster and eggs he was eating for breakfast, but he stopped eating as soon as we arrived at the table.

"I'm sorry about what happened to Zion, I loved him like a brother," Campa said.

"Thank you," I replied, unsure of what else to say.

"I brought you here to show you that we take care of ours. Come with me," Campa said, standing and leading the way into the house.

Tony gestured for me to follow, and he fell into step behind me. Under different circumstances, I might've been impressed by my surroundings, but none of this fancy shit meant a damn thing, because no amount of money would bring my man back. We boarded an elevator and took it down, but I was surprised to see that the basement didn't have the same lavish appeal as everything I'd see so far. It was dark and had a dark feel to it, almost like a wine cellar in the country. Campa opened the first door to the left of the elevator and ushered both of us inside. What I saw as soon as I crossed the threshold threatened the numbness I was feeling, because my confusion was instant, followed quickly by an anxiety I couldn't explain.

"Wh-what's this?" I asked, looking first at Campa and then at the three men, chained to the wall like they were in the dungeon of a castle.

"These are the men responsible for your husband laying in the city morgue right now," Campa replied, pulling a chrome Ruger .45 from his waistline and chambering a round.

The three black men were all tall, slim, and clearly angry even in the face of death. Not one man was shedding a tear for what they'd taken from me, nor did anyone show any sign of remorse. I didn't have to ask Campa how this would end for them though, and that gave me a little consolation.

"Thank you," I said, looking at Campa.

"You're more than welcome," he replied, extending his pistol towards me.

I looked at Tony, expecting to find the same expression of confusion on his face as I was wearing, but it wasn't there, and neither was there any surprise.

"I don't, I don't understand," I said slowly.

"What's not to understand? They took Zion from you, so what are you gonna do about it?" Campa asked.

"I thought you or one of your people—"

"Are you telling me, me and my people had more love and loyalty for Zion than *you* do?" Campa asked, slowly taking his sunglasses off and revealing his surprisingly dark eyes.

Looking him in the eyes made me seriously question if he had a soul at all, but in the grand scheme of things, that question wasn't important. I was clearly being put to the test, and I wasn't feeling like failure was an option. I knew there was no use looking at Tony for advice, because the sympathy he'd shown me a short while ago was now tucked away. There was no place for that here. I took the gun from Campa's extended hand and turned to face the three sets of eyes looking at me.

"That bitch ain't got it in her," the man in the middle said, snickering.

Without a word, I stepped up to him, put the barrel of the gun under his chin, and pulled the trigger. Something about seeing his brains stick to the ceiling calmed part of me and made me breathe a little easier. I quickly turned the gun on the man to my right, pressed the still-smoking barrel to his temple and pulled the trigger. The sound of Campa's laughter was echoing off the walls, but I ignored it as I moved directly in front of the last man on the hit parade.

"Pl-please, I didn't kill him, I didn't—"

I emptied the rest of the clip into his mouth, feeling more invigorated with every bullet that left the fun.

"Nice job, nice job," Campa said, clapping his hands and smiling widely.

It seemed stupid to say thank you, so I simply wiped my prints off the gun and passed it back to him.

"Nah, you keep that, it's my gift to you and a symbol of our new relationship," Campa replied.

"Relationship?" I asked.

"Yeah. You work for me now."

Aryanna

Chapter 4

"What exactly do you mean I work for you now?" I asked slowly.

"Come back upstairs and I'll explain. Tony, clean up this mess," Campa ordered, leading the way back to the door we entered.

My eyes briefly met Tony's, and he gave me a slight nod of approval that helped to slow the rolling of my stomach. The rush of adrenaline racing through my bloodstream was as real and intoxicating as it was scary. I'd never killed a man before, and to have gone from a virgin to having three bodies under my belt seemed unreal. I followed Campa in a slight daze, still feeling the weight of the gun in my hand, but not believing what it now represented. I was Zion's wife, his partner in all the ways that truly mattered, but this part of his life was only open to me to a certain point. Somehow, I knew that was forever about to change.

"Would you like something to eat?" Campa asked, reclaiming his seat at the patio table.

"No, I'm not hungry."

He gestured for me to sit down and I took the seat across from him, sitting the gun on the table.

"How much do you know about what your husband did for me?"

"Enough to know he'd never filed a tax return."

My comment made him laugh.

"That is very true, although the drug game does pay a heavy tax to this government in order for business to continue flourishing. That's how it's always been, and that's how it'll always be. Zion sold drugs for me, but he wasn't a corner boy, he was a serious earner. With him being gone now, it kinda leaves a hole in my operation, and I believe you're the person to fill it."

"Why me? I don't know anything about the dope game. I'm pretty sure you've got better qualified people to handle your business," I replied.

"All of that may be true, but I know you can handle it. You're a strong and capable woman, plus I think you'll succeed, based on what it would all mean to you from a sentimental standpoint."

"I appreciate your confidence in me, but I can't."

"You can and you will. What just happened downstairs was your job interview and I was impressed enough to hire you on the spot. That means you have two choices, Claudette. We can either discuss how things will go to ensure we have a smooth working relationship, or I can take you back downstairs to our human resources department to discuss your termination."

Had this been a Fortune 500 company, his proposal would've sounded purely rational, maybe even a little generous, but this wasn't that type of company. There were no fish in these water, only sharks. Evaluating it like that made my decision little more than a formality at this point.

"What is it you want me to do?" I asked.

"Pick up where your husband left off. Tony will assist you, but your learning curve has to be quick, because every day we're not running at mass production means we're losing money."

"And what exactly is mass production?" I asked.

"For you, it'll be about ten kilos a week to start off with, and then the numbers will depend on how well you apply yourself. Tony will show you the ins and outs, but you'll still be expected to maintain your normal life, in order to keep up your appearances. It might not hurt for you to consider attending law school on an actual campus to increase your clientele, acquire favors, and be seen."

It was an effort to keep my expression neutral at the mention of my education. In part, because the fact that this man obviously knew a lot about me was unsettling, but also because talking about school made me think about the conversation I'd had with Zion on that particular topic. I couldn't help wondering what he'd think if he could see me now, and that thought had the feeling of tears prickling the backs of my eyes.

"I'll need some time to mentally prepare. I'm sure you can understand that," I said.

"I can. Take a few days and bury your beloved, and Tony will be in touch with you."

The mention of the man's name brought him out of the house and towards us almost like magic.

"I made the call, Jefe, somebody will be here shortly," Tony said.

"Good. You can take Claudette home now, and then take care of that remaining business."

Tony nodded his head in understanding, and realizing I'd been dismissed, I stood up to leave.

"Don't forget your gift," Campa said, nodding towards the pistol on the table.

I picked it up and simply stared at it in my hand for a moment, wondering if it was my gift or my curse. Somehow, I knew that was only a question that could be answered with time. I tucked the gun into the back of my shorts and followed Tony back out to his car.

"Did you know that was gonna happen?" I asked, once we were inside and pulling away.

"I had a feeling, but I knew you could handle yourself."

I turned in the seat to look at him.

"How did you know I could handle myself in that situation though?"

"Because Zion never would've married you if you were weak, plus I've seen the damage you've done to him after a few of your more heated arguments. I've always known you possessed a strength inside you that if tapped into right, would bring out the savage side that's in all of us."

I contemplated his words as we rode on in silence, reflecting on the times I'd had to swing on Zion. In the moment, I'd been too angry to be terrified and afterwards, I'd been too consumed by us making up to care. Thinking about it now though made me smile because somehow, even in those tense moments, Zion had loved me beyond anything I'd ever dreamed possible. I would always cherish that, and now that I was walking in his footsteps, I'd be sure to make him proud.

"I know you've got shit to handle, but do you think you can go with me to the morgue so that…so that I can do what's necessary?" I asked.

"Of course."

The gratitude I felt didn't numb the pain creeping around my heart, but I doubted anything ever would. This loss would resonate with me until I took my last breath, but it would serve as motivation for everything else I did. It took us twenty minutes to get to the morgue, but the ten minutes I had to spend inside seemed twice as long. As badly as my mind and heart didn't want to accept Zion was truly dead, I couldn't convince myself that he was simply sleeping on the cold metal table. He was still beautiful in death, at least to me. I'd been grateful for Tony's presence, but I had one more favor to ask of him and I waited until we were back in the car before speaking on it.

"I need to do something, and I need your help."

"What do you need?" he asked without hesitation.

"The men I killed, which one of them was actually the trig-german?"

"The one who ran his mouth and ended up catching the first bullet from your gun."

"Does he have a family?"

My question made him pause and look at me out the corner of his eye while he continued driving.

"No family, just a wife. Why?"

"I need you to take me to see her."

"That's not a good idea, Claudette. You don't need to be seen with her, just in case some questions are asked later."

"Who's gonna ask questions? I'm pretty sure that in Campa's line of work, he has very efficient ways of making a body disappear, so her husband's death won't bring any ques-tions."

"You're right, but her death will. The remaining business Campa mentioned before we left was the elimination of eve-ryone's families."

Hearing this left me in silent contemplation for a moment, but in the end, it changed nothing about how I felt.

"Take me to her house, Tony. I don't care what you do when it comes to everybody else, but I need to see her face-to-face."

I could feel his hesitation, but he nodded in agreement an-yway. I laid back in the seat and thought about what I wanted to say to this woman when the time came. An hour later, Tony eased his car to the curb in front of a single-level family home, signaling that the time had come to speak my mind.

"You sure about this?" he asked.

"Yeah."

"Okay then, let's go," he said, opening his door and step-ping out.

I followed his lead all the way to the front door, but when he raised his fist to knock, I grabbed his arm to stop him.

"I got it," I said, stepping around him and knocking.

Within seconds, I could hear movement and suddenly the door was pulled open. The short Spanish chick standing in front of me was beautiful and her body looked right in the tight jeans and wife beater she had on. We were about the same height, but it wouldn't have mattered how big this bitch was. As soon as she opened her mouth to speak, I fired a jab to her nose, and quickly followed up with a fierce right hook that pushed her back into the house. She recovered quick and threw her hands up, but the sight of my gun winking at her made it clear that this was in no way a fair fight. I swiftly moved all the way into the house, and I heard Tony close the door behind us.

"Move," I said, gesturing with my gun towards the hallway behind her.

The fury in her brown eyes spoke to her desire to try me, but she knew better.

"You have no idea who you're fucking with, because my husband—"

"Your husband is dead, bitch, killed with this gun right here in my hand. You're about to join him, now move," I growled, taking a step towards her.

A number of different emotions swam through her eyes, but she backpedaled instead of acting on any of them. The hallway led to the kitchen at the back of the house and once we got there, I had to decide what to do next.

"Get on your knees and open your mouth," I demanded.

Her stare immediately skated past me to Tony's imposing figure, and I knew what she was thinking. After a moment's hesitation, she complied though. I stepped up to her and shoved my pistol in between her lips roughly, but I didn't speak at first, I simply stared at her with all the hatred I felt radiating through my body.

"Your-your husband took everything from me last night. He killed my husband. He took him from me! He took my son's father from him! And for what? What was it all about? Your husband probably thought it was just part of the dope game, and he was probably right. This is part of that same game, but this is the colder part. My husband believed that when you eliminated an enemy, you had to kill everything close to him. When you see him on the other side, tell him I sent you."

I pulled the trigger, sending her body sliding across the kitchen's linoleum floor. I kept my gun pointed in her direction in case she moved again, but when she didn't, I tucked it back into my shorts and turned to face Tony.

"We can go now."

"Yes, Mrs. Snow."

Even after we were back in the car and on the move, we remained silent, no doubt having similar thoughts for different reasons. Losing Zion had broken something in me, but for the sake of our son I knew that I couldn't allow it to break me. I knew now that the old Claudette was laying in the arms of the man she loved, in whatever afterlife existed far beyond this time and space. Who I would become was a mystery to me.

"I'll check on you in a few days," Tony said, once we'd pulled up in front of my house.

I nodded and got out of the car. My heart was heavy as I walked to my front door, but my determination carried me forward. As soon as I stepped in the house, I heard my son's footsteps approaching rapidly and within seconds, he bent the corner at high speed.

"Mama!" I opened my arms and scooped him off his feet, holding him close and inhaling his scent, as tears slid down my face.

Chapter 5

Five years later

"Mom, I'm not going to school today."

The sound of his voice forced my eyes open, even though I felt like I'd just opened them. Standing next to my bed was my late husband's miniature twin, looking every bit as determined as his daddy used to when it came to getting his way.

"Are you really about to start your shit today, Junior?"

"Why can't you just call me Zion like everybody else?"

How did I explain to him that just the mention of the name he shared with his dad still caused me pain? How was it fair of me to mention it? Good parents put their kid's needs before their own, right?

"Okay, Zion, are you really about to make me get ugly with you this early in the damn morning?"

"Why would you...unless you forgot what today is."

The look on his face told me that I better not have forgotten what today is, and that sent my brain spinning. The truth was, I hadn't forgot what today was, but I tended to block it from my mind because it was bittersweet.

"I know it's your birthday, boy, but I've gotta be in court in a little while, which means you gotta go to school."

"But, Mom, you never make me go to school on my birthday. You always give me a choice because that's what my dad would do, and it's his birthday too."

I'd always thought it was God's sense of humor to give me two men to love and celebrate on the same day, but did he really have to make them so much alike? Stubborn, logical, and unable to forget shit.

"Zion, I can't miss court."

"I'm nine years old now, Mom, that means you don't have to hover over me. Besides, you've got the entire house and property rigged with more security cameras than the White House!"

"You're nine, not nineteen, which means you have no business being home alone."

"Mom, with all the security and staff, how would I ever really be alone? Are you just putting up a fight because you actually did forget today was my birthday, and you need time to get my presents? If that's it, you can just tell me, and I'll understand."

His accusation and analyzation made me laugh softly as I thought about the amazing trial lawyer he'd make one day. For him to only be nine years old, he possessed an uncanny wisdom and intellect that had drawn both praise and criticism from his teachers. At parent/teacher conferences I encouraged the praise and made sure they knew to keep that other shit to themselves. Zion was my baby and he was perfect, even if he did get on my damn nerves with the bullshit sometimes.

"Go look in the garage, smartass," I said.

The way his eyes lit up made the hassle he was putting me through worth it. He made a mad dash from the room, knowing what could only be waiting for him in the garage. I stretched leisurely before pulling the covers back, climbing out of my comfortable king-sized bed, and making my way to the bathroom. The fog of sleep clung to me, making me regret having drinks with Tony after dinner. It wasn't every day we made a free million dollars though, so there was nothing wrong with toasting success. Domonique had tried to play me by unloading my almost pure product on the competition for a higher price, and then he had the nerve to stall with the payment! Killing the competition and reclaiming my product hadn't bothered me, but Domonique's betrayal had pissed me off enough to handle him accordingly. One of the many lesson's I'd learned from my husband was you didn't accept a loss, just because a lesson came with it. You taught a lesson of your own. After locking myself in the bathroom, I turned on the jets to my Jacuzzi tub, and waited on it to fill with hot water. While that was taking place, I grabbed my favorite dildo from under the sink. I'd had it made purely from the memory of Zion's dick that was permanently embedded on my brain, and the best part was that it stuck to any surface. This allowed me to take dick from multiple angles and positions, and this was the only thing besides my fingers that had been inside me in five years. I still belonged to my husband, mind, body, and soul. I quickly suctioned the toy to the side of the tub so that all eight inches stood tall like a chocolate birthday candle. I straddled it, opening my pussy to its invasion as I closed my eyes, and pictured the love of my life beneath me. My movements were similar to doing squats, only I wasn't worried about the burning in my legs because my pussy was already tingling. With my eyes still closed, I took ahold of my titties and squeezed them gently, while my fingers teased my nipples into painful hardness. In my mind, Zion's lips and tongue danced with my nipples as his dick throbbed wildly inside me, and that made me wetter. The kaleidoscope of images razing through my mind had my breathing ragged as they forced me to move faster. I was literally chasing a ghost, and the trembling in my legs told me I was hot on his muthafuckin heels. My pussy was wetter and hotter than the almost-full tub and the way it was pounding signaled the finish lane.

"I l-love you, Zion!" I moaned passionately, cumming fast and hard like a rogue wave.

The orgasm that rocked me was so powerful, it forced me up off the toy and had me sliding into my hot bath like soft bubbles across its surface. I took my time catching my breath, reclining beneath the water while it worked its magic on my body. I could hear the faint sounds of a small engine roaring to life, signaling Junior finding either his dirt bike or his go-cart, and I smiled. There was no doubt that I spoiled him, but he was a good kid and I believed in rewarding him for that. I had no doubt his daddy would've done the same thing, and that's why he got at least two extravagant gifts every year. I was already secretly dreading his fifteenth and sixteenth birthdays, because he'd probably end up with four very expensive cars. Some parents saw it as fundamentally wrong to indulge in the whims and wants of their children, because the world wouldn't bow to them in that manner. I knew my kid was different though, and I believed in treating him that way because one day, he would make the world bow to him. He was too much like his daddy not to. I spent a leisurely twenty minutes soaking in my tub before bathing myself and climbing out. I made sure to hide the evidence of my morning pleasure session, and then I set about preparing for the day in front of me. I chose a navy-blue Gucci pantsuit that hugged my curves seductively, no bra or panties, and some four-inch Gucci heels to match. I was beyond stingy with the pussy, but I sold sex with the same effortlessness that I did mass quantities of cocaine and marijuana. My attire always fitted my status as one of the few successful queen pins in American history, and the transition into a court of law was seamless. Once I was dressed, and smelling good enough for anyone to wanna eat, I made my way downstairs where I found my usual breakfast of turkey bacon and scrambled eggs waiting for me. I still loved to cook, but it seemed like there was never enough time in the day for all that. No sooner had I sat down at the kitchen table, I heard the doorbell ring, but the way the door quickly opened told me who it was.

"I'm surprised you're up this early," I said, looking at a slightly disheveled Tony coming into the kitchen.

"I forgot to leave Junior's present here when I dropped you off, and I wanted to bring it to him before he went to school."

"Oh, he's decided he's not going to school today because it's his birthday, and he knows I won't make him."

Tony simply smiled at hearing this, as he took a seat across from me while signaling the cook to bring him a plate of food. I knew he wouldn't do anything except side with Zion, because as his godfather, they were thicker than thieves and twice as crooked. No matter how many arguments I lost to the two of them, I never got mad, I was simply forever grateful for all Tony had done for us over the last five years. My connect had instructed Tony to show me the ropes of the business, but Tony's loyalty to my husband had allowed him to become the best friend I'd needed. We'd travelled through hell together more than once, and never dishonored Zion by taking it beyond true friendship. To put it simply, Tony had become a lifeline that I wouldn't have survived without, and I was eternally grateful for that.

"So, what did you get the birthday boy?" I asked, digging into my food.

"A drone."

Hearing this made me chuckle and shake my head at the same time.

"Did you not know he wanted a drone, or did you tell him he couldn't have one?"

"It's neither of those things. I was just wondering if you'd bought him a birthday present, or if you were already preparing him to inherit the family business," I replied.

The sheepish expression that covered the big man's face said it all, but the truth only made me laugh. While I fully believed in protecting my child's innocence, I didn't advocate him being ignorant to how the world truly worked, because that would only hurt him when it came time for him to step into his own. Technology was absolutely the future, so him knowing how to operate a drone was important. The fact that we used drones for a number of reasons in my business only worked to his advantage, if he decided this was the path he wanted to travel. Thankfully, that decision was years off, which meant all my baby boy had to do for now was be the amazing kid he was. The rest would handle itself.

"What time do you have to be in court?" Tony asked.

A quick look at my watch revealed the truth about time flying.

"In about forty-five minutes, but hopefully it doesn't last long. What do you got planned?"

"Nothing really, I guess I'll just hang out here with Junior until you get back."

"Just make sure that you eat something and wash last night off of you because you look rough bruh."

"Thanks for the compliment sis, you're a real asshole."

I chuckled again before eating some more of my food. By the time I'd cleaned my plate, Junior came rushing into the kitchen and ran straight into my arms.

"Thanks, Mom, you're the best!"

"Well, I'm glad you think so, but you know the rules. You stay within the gates of this community or on our property, and you don't let none of your little friends ride your shit. Their parents can't afford the same toys I provide for you."

"I know, Mom. Alexia is staying home from school too though, so I told her I'd give her a ride on the back of my dirt bike."

The way he blushed when speaking Alexia's name always made me smile, even as it broke my heart a little. I didn't want my baby boy to grow up, but the attention he paid the ten-year-old, half-black/half-Spanish girl next door told me that he was in fact, growing into a young man. I prayed every night for a few more years of little kid innocence, especially when it came to girls. The look Tony was giving me told me he understood the transitional period his godson was stepping into.

"The only way Alexia is getting on that bike with you is if her parents agree, and she has a helmet on," Tony said.

"But Mom has court, so—"

"So, it's a good thing I don't, which means I can have the necessary conversation with her parents. Let's go handle that."

I fought to keep a straight face as Junior rolled his eyes dramatically, before kissing me on the cheek and following Tony out of the kitchen. I could only imagine how difficult he was gonna be as a teenage boy chasing after pussy, but thankfully that was years off. After grabbing my travel mug full of French vanilla coffee, I gathered my things and headed for the garage. Once I was behind the wheel of my silver G550 Mercedes truck, I made sure the Glock .23 I kept in between my seat and the center console was fully loaded. I performed the same check on the Ruger .380 I kept in the glove compartment, and then I got on the move. It didn't matter where I went, I never left my house unarmed. Every vehicle I owned was bulletproof and on most occasions, I travelled within a small motorcade of vehicles that blended effortlessly with the melting pot known as Miami. I wasn't simply cautious. I was paranoid and proud of it. The scars on my face came from shattered glass, courtesy of the flying bullets of rivals, and those scars reminded me that paranoid had saved my life up to this point. I saw no reason to change. It took me half an hour to make it into downtown Miami, which left me fifteen minutes to spare before my 8:30 am court appearance. I used the time to quickly go over my paperwork before I made my way into the courthouse.

"Good morning, Mrs. Snow," my paralegal Marsha said.

I took the folder she was offering me in exchange for the briefcase and coffee in my hands.

"New client?"

"Yes ma'am, no recommendation either," she replied.

Most of my clients were referred to me simply because my name moved with equal respect in both circles of life, and for the same reasons I got clients that came to me because of my reputation. I proceeded with caution when it came to these types, simply because their motivation for seeking me out had to be evaluated and reevaluated. I flipped open the folder and stared at the mugshot of the gorgeous Dominican woman named Phillisa. Her rap sheet was extensive, and the sparkle in her eyes didn't conceal the killer instinct I'd come to recognize at a glance.

"Conspiracy to distribute, huh? So, who's she pushing for?" I asked, soft enough not to be overheard.

"She wanted to discuss all business with you in person."

I followed Marsha's look to the benches that lined the hall outside the courtrooms, quickly spotting Phillisa sitting quietly among the crowd. The power she exuded was obvious, but so were the four goons that stood no more than three feet from her on any side.

"Is her court date today?" I asked.

"No, but she insisted on meeting with you immediately, and I told her you'd be here all day."

I glanced at my watch as I passed Marsha the folder back and took my coffee. I sipped from my mug thoughtfully while staring at the woman staring back at me, liking the fact that she was confident enough to size me up to my face. I gave her a slight nod, to which she responded by standing up and stepping away from her security to come to me.

"I don't know you," I stated calmly.

"No, you don't, but Zion was family to me."

Aryanna

Chapter 6

Her use of my husband's name was like a kick to the stomach, but I showed no outward signs of distress as I sipped from my coffee cup slowly.

"Marsha, give us a minute."

Without hesitation, she stepped away from us and I took a half a step closer to Phillisa to make sure she was the only one to hear me speak.

"You've obviously heard of me, but I will still give you a fair warning. Watch how you speak my husband's name."

I knew the look accompanying my statement ensured I didn't need to elaborate on my threat, and her slight smile told me that she got the message loud and clear.

"Even if I didn't need your help, I still wouldn't speak disrespectfully about Zion, nor would I disrespect you for no reason, Mrs. Snow."

"How old are you?"

"I'm twenty-three, why?" she replied, puzzled but amused by my question.

"So, that would mean you were eighteen when Zion died. A kid."

"Eighteen yes, but I haven't been a kid since I was old enough to understand what my uncle's drinking would lead him to do to me late at night. My wisdom can't be measured by age, only by experience, because I've got a lot of that. Zion was something like my mentor when I first started out in the game, and I feel like he's the reason I'm still alive today."

I didn't immediately respond to what she'd said, instead choosing to let it roll around my brain and soak in. Truthfully, her words weren't important, because as a lawyer I knew words were nothing more than tools of manipulation used to serve the self-interests of whoever was slinging them. That's why if you really wanted to hear what someone was saying to you, you had to hear what was behind the words, and often take it deeper by listening to the truths spoken through silence. People always told you who they were, the question was, were you listening or waiting to talk, which allowed you to miss what was said.

"There's a restaurant not far from here where we can discuss business privately. I'll be tied up here in court for the next few hours, but I can meet you there for lunch. Let's say at about two pm."

"I appreciate you taking the time for me. I'll be there."

The fact that she turned and walked away without asking me for the restaurant's name or directions to it left me with mixed emotions. Her actions made it somewhat obvious she was familiar with both me and Zion, since the restaurant we'd be meeting at was one that he'd owned. To my knowledge, not a lot of people had known that five years ago, and I kept my ownership of it a closely guarded secret, because it held more sentiment than anything. If nothing else, Phillisa's knowledge had me intrigued.

"Everything good, boss?" Marsha asked, coming back to my side.

"Yeah, just make sure we have all available information on her."

"I'll get that for you right away."

I reclaimed my briefcase and headed into the courtroom to begin the days battle. Selling dope had become a surprise outlet for the darkness in me but becoming a trial lawyer was the therapeutic balance I needed to live. Inside the walls of a courtroom, I got to achieve the things money can't buy, and I got to give light to the intellect my husband loved so much. Every case I took, I viewed it as another opportunity to make Zion proud, because he'd always encouraged me to be who

I'd become. At least as it pertained to being a lawyer. I quickly made my way to the defense table and began to set up shop. Ten minutes later, the bailiff led my client in, and sat her in the chair next to me. Brenda Stansfield looked like nothing more than the white, all-American housewife, in her loose-fitting summer dress, but I knew there was a reason she was currently on trial for killing her husband. Luckily for her, she had friends in the right places, and a daddy who knew politicians, so she got the best help money and a favor could buy. I never took a high-profile case without making sure a favor was included in the arrangements for payment. Money was appreciated, but it couldn't buy everything, so I took my cue from Vito Corleone.

"How are we looking?" Brenda asked softly.

It was always the same question from her whenever I'd see her. Naturally, people were nervous when they were on trial for their life, no matter how good the lawyer was sitting beside them. Brenda's situation was different though because we both knew she'd actually done what she was accused of. It couldn't be proven though.

"We're good, nothing has changed."

My response sounded benign to anyone listening, but between us we knew it meant there was still no proof Brenda's husband was even dead. Murder was still damn near impossible to prove without a body, and not even a miracle could bring Brenda's husband back from his final resting place. The only reason she'd ended up charged was because of circumstantial evidence in the form of her husband's blood on the rear bumper of her car, and a history of domestic violence between the two of them. Times had definitely changed, because little white women weren't getting their asses whooped anymore, they were whooping ass too. Out of my peripheral vision, I saw the prosecutor come in and go to his table. When I turned my full attention on him, I found him staring intently at me, with a piece of paper clutched in his grip. I was more curious than nervous about what had him looking at me with such defiance, but before I could say anything, he came from around his desk and walked over to the bailiff. They exchanged a few words, he handed the bailiff the paper, and returned to the seat behind his table.

"Mrs. Snow, what's happening?" Brenda asked.

"I'm not sure, but I promise there's nothing to worry about."

I knew the smoothness of the lie off my tongue would serve to stabilize her, but my attention was now on the bailiff who was disappearing from sight. I really didn't have a clue as to what was going on, but I knew better than to let them see me sweat, so I continued unpacking my things. As I was preparing to sit down beside Brenda and review some things I'd jotted down, the bailiff remerged and summoned me to follow him. When I saw him do the same thing to the prosecutor, I felt the tingling of unease working its way up my spine.

"Mrs. Snow—"

"Just sit tight, Brenda, I'll be right back," I said, following both men out of the courtroom.

The bailiff led us to the chambers of the Honorable Judge Naomi Powers and left us alone with her. The judge looked at us and then she scanned the paper in her hands, which I recognized as the one the prosecutor had sent with the bailiff.

"Counselor Billings, am I reading this motion correctly? You wish to drop the charges against Brenda Stansfield?"

"Without prejudice, Your Honor. While the state does believe Mrs. Stansfield killed her husband and disposed of the body, we're not fully prepared to present our case in a way that would yield the desired outcome. So yes, we would like to drop the charges at this point, but should new evidence arise, we will move forward."

"New evidence? You mean like the actual body for the man you're claiming my client killed?" I asked sarcastically.

I could tell by the way his jaw clenched that I was under his skin, and that made me smile. Troy Billings wasn't the first white man's feathers I'd ruffled, nor would they be the first I'd plucked in a court of law.

"Mrs. Snow, do you have any objections to the state's motion?" Judge Powers asked.

"No, Your Honor."

"Then I will grant it and order the immediate release of your client."

With that decided, the judge swiftly scribbled her signature on the document she was holding, and that signaled the conclusion of our meeting. I wanted to gloat as I followed the prosecutor out of the judge's chambers and back into the courtroom, but I kept it professional instead. I could see the worry etched into every line on Brenda's face, but when she saw me smiling, she visibly relaxed.

"Is everything okay?"

"It's better than okay, and you're about to find out what I mean, so just sit still and wait," I replied, taking her hand as I reclaimed the seat next to her.

A few moments later, the judge's arrival was announced, and after everyone stood to greet her, we sat back down so the show could begin. The announcement came quick like ripping a band-aid off, causing the courtroom to erupt with murmurs of disbelief from both sides of the aisle. For a second, Brenda was too stunned to speak and then the tears came, followed quickly by her hugging me and saying thank you over and over again.

"Just keep your head down for a while, because they'll be watching you," I whispered in her ear.

She agreed to do just that, and after I explained that she had to be processed out of the jail system, she happily went along with the deputy. I quickly repacked my briefcase and made my exit through the side door to avoid any questions from anyone. It felt good to get the win, but I still had more work to do today. The next four hours passed in a haze of plea bargains, oral arguments and trial dates rescheduled and by the time it was all done, I was back to regretting my late night with Tony. I was more than thankful that I was done for the day by the time the courts shut down for lunch, even though I wasn't technically done working. I still had to check on a few things for my more lucrative business, but my first stop was my restaurant, Food For The Soul. I parked out back and made sure to conceal my Glock .23 on me, before I got out and made my way inside through the kitchen. I went straight to my office to access the live camera feed I had running throughout the entire restaurant, and I took my time observing who was in my establishment. Our menu offered a wide variety of food, which attracted all different types of clientele. Normally, I just took the time to people watch because it was a good way to learn more than the subconscious wanted to reveal. As soon as I spotted Phillisa though, I headed out onto the restaurant floor to meet her.

"Enjoying your meal?" I asked, taking the seat across from her.

"The food here is always delicious. That's why I make it a point to come here on date night."

"I see. And how exactly do you know about this restaurant?" I asked.

"Back when it was called Mario's, Zion had to take a meeting here, and I was a part of the team he'd brought with him."

"So, you're a shooter, or..."

I let my sentence train off, wanting her to fill in the blanks so I could gauge how much truth came before the lies.

"I was whatever Zion needed me to be. Shooter, mule, driver, whatever."

"That sounds like a whole lot of loyalty on your part. Why did my husband deserve that from you?"

"Because he gave that. I don't have to tell you who Zion was, because you know him probably better than anyone, so you know he was a real nigga. Those are hard to find, so when you're lucky enough to cross paths with one, you follow him into hell without question or hesitation."

Despite the calmness she spoke with, I could still see the pain of loss in her eyes, and it pulled at me enough to consider helping her.

"Just because you knew my husband, doesn't mean I'm doing you any favors."

She flashed a smile at me before signaling one of her men, a few tables away. Without a word, he approached us and handed her a briefcase before returning to his seat. She passed the case to me, and I opened it to find a hard drive.

"I'm sure you're familiar with crypted currency, Mrs. Snow. There's a million dollars on that hard drive and it's yours, whether you take my case or not. I just want you to hear me out."

"Start talking."

Aryanna

Chapter 7

Despite my mind being preoccupied, I thought my heart might come out of my chest as I pulled into my driveway and caught sight of Junior, wheeling his dirt bike up the street in my direction. Somehow, I managed not to scream my fool head off, but I was out of my truck before my wheels had completely stopped rolling. I immediately spotted Tony and Alexia sitting out front of my house, enjoying the show my son was putting on, but that didn't stop me from signaling for him to bring his little ass to me.

"Hey, Mom, did you see—"

"I saw you and if I catch you doing that shit again, you'll park that bike until you're sixteen," I stated angrily.

"But Mom, I—"

"I don't wanna hear it, Zion! You ain't no stunt rider, and that helmet ain't gonna prevent you from getting seriously hurt if that bike falls on your little ass. Keep both wheels on the ground, understood?"

The flash of fire that raced through his eyes made him look more like his dad than anything else ever could, but he knew to suppress the urge to say or do anything stupid. Out of my peripheral vision, I could see Tony and Alexia moving towards us, and I felt bad for embarrassing him. Only a little though.

"I understand, Mom."

The sullen tone of his voice pulled at my heart strings, but it was important to me that he know how serious his safety was.

"What do you want for dinner?" I asked gently.

The way he hunched his shoulders and avoided eye contact made it clear he was still in his feelings, but I knew how to fix that.

"Alexia, would you like to join us for dinner, if it's okay with your parents?" I asked.

"Yes ma'am."

"Okay. Junior, why don't you take her to her house so she can make sure it's okay, and then come back so you can help me with something."

"You want me to help you cook my own birthday dinner?"

The look of righteous indignation on his face made me chuckle, but instead of responding, I opened the back door to my truck, and pulled out a bag.

"I need your help setting this up."

The sight of the PlayStation box sticking up through the bag quickly transformed his expression from upset to pure joy. It took him three tries to get the dirt bike on its kickstand so he could hop off it and rush into my arms, making me laugh as he said thank you over and over.

"You're welcome, now take it in the house and then go do what I asked you, so Alexia can stay for dinner."

He quickly took the bag and dashed in the house, reappearing moments later with his go-cart to scoop Alexia up.

"That's a preview of the years to come," Tony said, watching them take off down the street.

"Don't remind me. How did things go here today?"

"Quiet, until Hurricane Claudette blew in and went off on the birthday boy. How was your day?"

"You know he's not experienced enough to be doing wheelies and shit, Tony, so don't go there because I should be cussing your ass out too."

"I'd like to remind you that today was not Zion's first time on a dirt bike and secondly, it was you who bought him the damn thing. You can act like you didn't know he was gonna try all the cool shit he's seen done, but you know your son. So, what are you really upset about, Claudette?"

"Losing him."

Tony knew me well enough that I didn't have to elaborate past those two words. I tried my hardest to be the "cool" mom, but the reality was that I often held on to my son too tight because the fear of losing him was something I'd lived with every second since his dad was snatched away from me. I didn't want to smother him, but it was a daily battle within myself I had to fight.

"You already know I would give my life for Junior's as quickly as you would, Claudette, so you should know I wouldn't let him be reckless or careless."

"I know."

We both knew that was the furthest I was gonna go when it came to admitting I slightly overreacted, so the topic was dropped as Tony pulled me towards him and let me into the house.

"Figure out what to have for dinner, because Zion and Alexia have been snacking all day so they wouldn't have to quit playing for long."

"I'm surprised you actually went for that. Let me find out you're getting soft, nigga."

"Nah, I just didn't wanna interrupt his first date with a girl."

Hearing this statement stopped my feet from moving, as I looked closely at him to see if he was just fucking with me.

"I'ma need you to rephrase that shit because my nine-year-old son is not dating."

"I hate to break it to you, sis, but he definitely likes Alexia, and she sees stars when she looks at him too."

I fought the rolling sensation in my stomach while continuing into the house. I made my way to the kitchen and took a seat at the table, resisting the urge to shoot Tony in the ass for laughing at my pain. I mentally refused to accept the information I'd just been given, instead choosing to focus on ordering all of Junior's favorite foods to be delivered. With that taken care of, I decided to use the few moments I had alone with Tony to discuss something of equal importance.

"What do you know about a Phillisa Toreno?"

"What should I know about her?" he replied, sitting across from me at the table.

"Well apparently, she's a mover and a shaker who's currently charged with conspiracy to distribute cocaine in mass quantity, but she doesn't work for us. According to her, she's partnered up with some serious players out of Medellín, despite the fact that she's from Miami."

"Columbians, huh? Well, that means she's pushing quality product, and that makes Phillisa the competition, so why would she come to you for legal representation? And why would you entertain her, Claudette?"

"Because she knew Zion."

His eyes suddenly got darker after hearing my response, and I could feel the anger rolling off of him in silent waves.

"Knowing Zion's name ain't the same as knowing him, so—"

"She knew about the restaurant. We just had a late lunch there, where she gave me a million dollars to do no more than listen to her story. You know as well as I do that very few people knew about Zion inheriting that restaurant, but she said she attended a meeting there before. She also said Zion was something like a mentor."

The color of Tony's eyes didn't shift again, but his expression definitely changed to one I couldn't decipher.

"How old is she?" he asked.

"Twenty-three, why?"

"Do you have a picture of her on you, or her file with all her info?"

"Tony, you know I've got my people doing a thorough background check, so I'm not coming to you for that. If this woman truly knows and was around Zion, then I can only assume she was around you, which means you would know the shit that's not gonna show up in black and white. I'm starting to get the feeling that you know something, and I'ma need you to tell me whatever it is."

For a moment he simply stared at me without saying a word, but his silence was screaming there was definitely something that needed to be verbalized. We both knew I could wait him out, but the longer he made me wait, the angrier I was gonna get. The sound of approaching footsteps hurrying in our direction was the only thing that saved his ass. It was only a temporary reprieve though.

"Alexia's parents said she could stay for dinner, and they thanked you for inviting her, Mom."

"Okay, baby, I ordered all of your favorite foods," I replied, without taking my eyes off Tony.

"What about a cake?" Alexia asked.

"I was just about to go get one, but I wanted to make sure the birthday boy was good with ice cream cake from Dairy Queen," Tony said, hopping up from his seat and turning his attention on the kids.

"Can you get one with mint chocolate chip ice cream in it?" Junior asked, licking his lips.

"I'll get two."

Junior quickly gave Tony a hug, and then the big man disappeared back up the hallway without a backwards glance in my direction. It was extremely tempting to shoot him in his ass, but I resisted the urge for the sake of the children. His ass couldn't duck me for long though.

"Mom can we hook up my PlayStation now?"

The excitement on my son's face pushed all other thoughts out of my mind as my heart beat with joy and sadness. There wasn't a moment that passed when I didn't wish Zion was here to see his son and enjoy his little kid innocence, but since he wasn't, I was determined to enjoy it for him.

"Yes, we can hook it up. Are we putting it in your room?"

"I was hoping you'd let me put it down here in the living room on the big screen," he replied, smiling sheepishly.

"I'll do you one better, let's hook it up in the movie room so that you can play it on the projection screen."

"Really, Mom?"

The excitement and disbelief covering his face made me laugh with delight as I opened my arms to receive his hug.

"You're the best, Mom!"

"Just remember that when I say or do something you don't like in the future."

The look he gave me said I could do no wrong, but we both knew I was the definition of overprotective.

"Grab the bag and meet me downstairs," I instructed.

Once they'd taken off in the direction of the living room, I pulled out my phone, and shot Tony a text to remind him to pick up balloons for us to release for my husband. I made sure to add that he needed to hurry his ass up too, because our conversation definitely wasn't over. With that done, I headed for the in-house movie theater I'd had built to bring Disney to life for my little man, preparing to now transform it into a partial man cave. Once the kids finally made it down there, we took everything out of the boxes and got to work. A half an hour into assembly, I realized I probably should've left this up to Tony, because I was lost like shit, but we were still having fun figuring it out. As the food started to arrive, we decided to have it brought in and set up downstairs with us, so that we could eat while we worked. I was just about to wonder where the fuck Tony was when I got a text from him, saying the cake was in the freezer, but Campa had summoned him to handle some business. If he hadn't spent all day with his godson, I would've been pissed by this interruption, and I probably would've called Campa myself. Today was an important day for family, but I knew in Campa's mind, his bottom line came before anything, so I simply replied to Tony's text that I understood. I didn't let it ruin my mood or the festivities, and once we finally got the PlayStation working, the fun went to the next level. I'd been smart enough to buy multiple controllers, which allowed all of us to play together at the same time. At first it was kinda concerning that a nine- and ten-year-old were kickin my ass at Fortnite, considering I was about that pistol play in real life. I got the hang of it though, and they eventually realized it was in their best interest to team up with me and fight other opponents around the world. It was easy to lose track of time, and I probably would've kept playing all night if it wasn't for the insistent ringing of my phone. I missed the call, but there were no less than ten texts from Campa, telling me to get to his house immediately.

"Fuck," I said aloud, sending him a quick text.

"What's wrong, Mom?"

"Nothing baby, I just have to go handle something at the restaurant real quick."

"Right now, though?"

I could tell by the way he asked that question, he wasn't happy our good time was interrupted for some work shit. I really didn't wanna go, but Campa's insistence made saying no impossible.

"I won't be gone long, sweetheart. You don't have to go to bed, and I'll let you stay home from school tomorrow if you want to."

"Can Alexia stay the night?" he asked, hopeful.

The answer on the tip of my tongue was *hell nah*, but I had to look at them for the kids that they were.

"Only if her parents okay it, and I need to hear them say that," I replied, passing my phone to Alexia.

She quickly dialed her number and put it on speaker phone so I could hear the entire exchange between her and her mom. After her mom gave her permission, I spoke briefly with her and her husband before disconnecting.

"Alright you two, I expect you to stay in this house and don't break anything. Junior you know what I expect, so don't make me embarrass you in front of your friend. Understand?"

"Yes, ma'am."

"Good talk, now give me a hug."

To my surprise, both of them hugged me before going back to the land of Fortnite. After getting with my security to make sure they knew what was going on I hopped in my gunmetal gray 2023 Aston Martin and got on the move. It only took me twenty-five minutes to get to Campa's house, and I wasn't surprised to find Tony's Ferrari parked in the driveway. I had no idea what this emergency meeting was about, but I hoped it didn't involve anything that would affect our money or product. It seemed like shit always went wrong when it was running smooth. The front door was opened before I had a chance to knock, and I was immediately led downstairs to the dungeon. It never got any easier to take this walk, despite the time that had passed since I performed my first executions here. Killing my husband's killers didn't bother me. But coming down here always forced me to remember why I'd killed them. Part of me expected to see those same three men strung up against the wall, but as I came through the door, I came face-to-face with something infinitely worse.

"Wh-what the fuck, Campa? Why is Tony strung up?"

Chapter 8

"Good of you to finally join us, Claudette. To answer your question, this disloyal, thieving, sneaky motherfucker is strung up because he had the balls to steal product from me. We'll see how many balls he had when I'm through with him though."

I could hear the words Campa was speaking, but their meaning wasn't computing to my brain. There was no way that Tony, my Tony, had stolen a damn thing from Campa! There had to be a mistake made somewhere, and I needed to figure this shit out before this went too far.

"Campa, you know Tony, so you know he would never steal anything from you. Where the hell did you get this crazy idea?" I asked, moving further into the room and closer to Tony.

"It's not an idea, and don't talk to me like I wouldn't have done my due diligence before I made a move, because I've been doing this shit a lot longer than you," he replied.

I could hear the agitation in his voice, and if the Glock .27 in his hand didn't signal the mood he was in, the destruction to Tony's face said it loud and clear.

"I'm not trying to insult you, Jefe, I'm simply saying that you know Tony. He's been with you the longest out of any of your employees, and his loyalty has never been called into question before now. What evidence do you have against him?"

"Ah, so you want to be his lawyer, Mrs. Snow? That's fine, we can have his trial here and now. The evidence I have against this piece of shit is the one and a quarter tons of coke I found in his house."

"A ton of coke? You tortured and beat Tony over a ton of cocaine…seriously?" I asked in disbelief.

71

"Is a ton of pure cocaine not worth tens of millions of dollars to us? I know you're not so rich that you would piss away millions without thinking of the consequences, so why do you expect me to do that?"

"I don't expect that, it's just that-I mean we deal with a lot of cocaine, so if Tony was gonna take something, don't you think he would take more?" I asked logically.

Tony suddenly started moaning loudly and when I turned my attention on him, I could tell he was nodding his head in agreement with what I was saying.

"You'll have to forgive his nonverbal communication. I cut his tongue out first so I didn't have to keep hearing his constant lies," Campa said smiling.

The chill I felt roll through my body continued until it reached my feet, and then it worked its way back up. This situation was beyond out of control and I had no idea how to get it back to normal.

"Campa, I don't understand what made you search Tony's house in the first place, and why didn't you tell me some product was missing?"

"I didn't know I was answering to you instead of it being the other way around, Mrs. Snow."

His voice was softer now than it had been a moment before, but I was familiar with the slight edge I could hear just beneath the surface. He was about tired of me questioning him, but I didn't know of another way to get to the bottom of this situation.

"Ok… Jefe, if you believe Tony did this then let me deal with him. This happened on my watch, so I will absorb the loss and make it right on the books," I offered.

"That's generous of you, Claudette, but how am I to know exactly how much product this sticky-fingered piece of shit has walked away with over the years? Are you willing to give up every dime you have?"

"If that's what it takes, then yes. I will," I replied without hesitation.

My response caused Campa to pause and stare at me silently for a few moments. When he smiled, I felt myself relax slightly because I knew this situation could've gone very bad very quick, but we'd avoided that thankfully. It took me a few seconds to realize the smile on Campa's face wasn't going all the way up to his eyes, and before I could say or do anything else, he raised the pistol in his hand and fired three shots. I stared at Tony in shock, not believing he had three holes in his chest, or that they were bleeding fiercely with his life's force.

"N-no. Nooo," I whispered, shaking my head slowly as tears sprang to my eyes and rolled down my face.

My movements to get to Tony weren't consciously made, but I found myself staring up into his now vacant stare, waiting on him to smile down at me like this was all a bad joke. When he didn't do that, I turned to look at Campa.

"Wh-why Campa? Why? I told you I'd give you whatever you wanted."

"What I want is employees I can trust and that's something money can't buy, so your money is of no use to me. Your loyalty is admirable though, and that's why I didn't shoot you along with him."

"Sh-shoot me?" I asked in complete disbelief.

"I won't lie, it crossed my mind because there was always the chance that you two were in on it together. I'm choosing not to believe that's the case though…don't make me regret that."

He stared at me for a second longer, before tucking his gun back into the waist of his white slacks and walking from the room like nothing at all had happened. It wasn't until he was gone that I took my first deep breath. I had to put my hand over my mouth to keep the scream trapped that was bubbling up from my throat, but I couldn't stop the tears that were now racing down my face. Tony wasn't just someone I worked with, he was literally my brother in every sense of the word, and I'd just watched him killed for no reason. There was nothing anyone could say that would ever convince me Tony had been stealing from Campa! So, either someone had set him up for this exact purpose, or Campa killed him for another reason that he didn't want me to know. All I knew at this point was my brother hadn't deserved to die.

"How do I go on now?" I asked softly, taking his still warm hand in my own.

I wanted so badly to hear his voice, to hear him laugh and say this was a horrible joke that they had played on me or something. I didn't want him to be dead, because he couldn't be dead. Junior and I needed him too much for him to be dead! I wouldn't have made it one day in the last five years without Tony, so it was impossible for me to see myself doing that now. The warmth of his hand made me look up into his face like I'd been blessed with a miracle, but his expression hadn't changed, and I knew in my heart it never would again.

"I-I love you. Always," I said, kissing his hand and touching it to my forehead one last time.

I spent a few more moments crying softly, and then I tucked my raw emotions away so I could go deal with the aftermath. I made my way back upstairs in a fog and went in search of Campa. I found him sitting out by the pool, getting a foot massage from a naked Spanish chick, while sipping an amber liquor in a glass.

"My brother didn't steal anything from you, because that would've meant he stole from me, so who told you there was product missing?"

"It doesn't matter, Claudette, I took care of it and now we can get back to work. For starters, I need you to tell Ms. Toreno you can't help with her legal troubles."

"How do you know about that?" I asked slowly.

"I know everything, Claudette, have you forgotten that already?"

Ordinarily, I didn't have a problem taking orders from Campa, because he'd single-handedly changed my life, and gave me the game on a different level. But something about this didn't sit well with me. Claudette Snow was nobody's puppet.

"I can't refuse to help her because I've already been paid and retained. The last thing I need is the scrutiny that comes with a board of ethics violation, and I would think you wouldn't want anyone paying that close of attention to me either."

I could tell by the look on his face that he didn't like being told no, but that was okay with me, because I didn't like the fact that someone I loved was dead in his damn cellar.

"Well, you will most certainly lose her case, and you will make it look believable, so you don't come under scrutiny for that. Am I making myself clear?"

"Si, Jefe. Is there any reason in particular that you care so much about my client?" I asked, looking pointedly at him.

"Your client is the competition, and you being of any assistance to her and her interests, means you're neglecting our interests. Do I need to explain to you why that's a bad thing...or would you like to discuss it with Tony?"

It took everything in me not to reach for my gun and permanently erase the smug smile off this motherfucker's face, but I somehow managed to keep a neutral expression.

"I see your point clearly, Jefe. Is there anything else you need from me?"

"No, that will be all for now. Oh, and you can have Tony's car if you want it. Matter of fact, give it to your son for his birthday, and tell him it came from his uncle Campa. I'll make sure that Tony's family gets the usual financial assistance afforded to a top earner of this organization," he replied, as if he were doing all of us a great favor.

"You don't have to worry about Tony's family, I'll take care of everything. Thank you though."

"No problem. You can show yourself out," he said, leaning back and closing his eyes.

He may have thought I was being sarcastic or disingenuous when I thanked him, but I actually meant what I'd said. He had taught me a very valuable lesson tonight that I would never forget, and it was a lesson I was sure he'd learn too one day. I quickly left him and his masseuse to their activities, but instead of heading outside to my car, I made a detour back downstairs to the dungeon. Past experience had taught me that Campa had many able hands to dispose of bodies once their souls had left them, but I refused to let Tony become just another pile of woodchips somewhere in the world. I'd made sure to swing past the kitchen and grab a knife so I could cut him down off the wall, but that was the easy part, because Tony wasn't a little nigga. Even as I pulled and tugged his body out of the room and up the stairs, I could feel the endless stream of tears rushing down my face, but I remained determined. It literally took sweat and tears to get his body upstairs and into the passenger seat of my car. I was covered in his blood by the time I got there, but I finally got him inside. I got behind the wheel of my car and pulled off, only to realize that I didn't know where I was headed. I couldn't just dump his body at the hospital, and it would've been pointless anyway, considering there was nothing anyone there could do. I couldn't take him home to his family either, because finding out they had just lost a loved one shouldn't happen with the body full of holes visible for their viewing. After driving around aimlessly for ten minutes, I grabbed my phone and made the only call that made sense.

"Is everything okay, Snow?" she asked, answering right away.

"No, and I can't explain why over the phone."

"I'm at the house, pull up on me," she said.

I hung up without saying another word, thankful that I had a good team behind me. Now that I had a direction to head in, it only took me fifteen minutes to get to my destination, and thankfully my girl was standing out front when I pulled up. I caught the concerned look in her brown eyes when my headlights flashed across her body, and I also saw the two-tone black .357 Ruger pistol she was concealing beside her leg. Morano, aka Mo-Mo, was part of the well-oiled machine I'd put together when it came to my team of go-getters in the street. She was a gorgeous, five-foot-six inch, one-hundred-sixty-pound Puerto Rican stallion, that had a quick smile, and a quicker trigger finger to match her temper. By day she was nothing more than a sergeant inside the Department of Corrections, but by night she was a killer and a hustler I could depend on for whatever. If there was ever a woman I would give the pussy up to, it was Mo and she knew it.

"What the fuck happened?" she asked once she'd leaned down into the car and spotted the bullet holes in Tony's chest.

"It's a long story, but I need your help."

"You know you don't have to ask twice. Come here," she said, pulling me out of the car and into her arms in one fluid motion.

My crying spell earlier was nothing compared to the gut-wrenching wails I let loose now. I cried from the depths of my soul for the brother I'd lost, and when I thought I was all cried out, I cried some more. By the time I'd gotten myself together, Mo had led me inside her house and sat with me on the couch so she could hold me close.

"He-he didn't do anything, Mo," I sobbed.

"Tell me what happened."

I took several deep breaths before I tried speaking again, still trying to wrap my mind around all that had happened inside of the last hour. It seemed unreal, but the blood on my hands and clothes was very real, and that made the situation undeniable. I recounted the events that had led to me sitting on her couch in her arms to the best of my ability, pausing a few times to get myself together. When I was done talking, she leaned back to look at me in the eyes.

"I agree with you, bae so the question is, how do you wanna handle it?"

Despite being emotionally exhausted, I smiled because this was why she was my motherfucking bitch. She would ride and die with me no matter who the opp was, and she knew Campa was a more than formidable opponent.

"I don't know what my next move is yet, but when I do, I'm definitely gonna need you," I replied.

"I'm all yours, Mrs. Snow."

Chapter 9

I didn't know how long I'd been in the shower, but the hot water hadn't faded in the slightest, and the pounding pressure that rained on my body felt better than good. I tried in vain to clear my thoughts, but every time I closed my eyes, I saw Tony's body and that forced more tears from my eyes. When I wasn't seeing his death, my mind shifted to my son, my precious innocent son, who would be devastated by the loss we'd suffered. Losing Zion had been hard for Junior to really comprehend at that young age, and by the time he was old enough to understand, some of the sting of what happened had dissipated. To lose Tony would hit differently though, because this was the one man who had been there for his whole life. No matter what the reason, issue, or situation, Tony had been there for both me and Junior, and I knew my little man was gonna take it just as hard as I was. Then for it to happen on his and his father's birthday…that was just cruelty on a different level! I'd been racking my brain, trying to figure out how the hell I was gonna tell him what had happened, but there were no words that wouldn't break his heart. All I could think to do right now was avoid the topic all together and hope to come up with a pretty lie before the ugly truth came out.

"Snow…you good in there?" Mo called from the other side of the bathroom door.

"No, but I'll be out in a minute."

I turned off the water and stepped out of the shower into the room full of steam while reaching for a towel. My movements were purely instinct, because the numbness that takes over to suppress the pain had officially moved in on me. I was thankful because I was so tired of crying, and this whole situation reminded me of how I'd been when I'd lost Zion. My love for Tony had been different, but I had loved him nonetheless and that meant I would be in pain for a long time. I knew what I had to do was channel my pain and my anger into constructive energy, so I didn't allow it to cause me to self-destruct. I had to keep pushing because that's what Tony expected of me. Given our chosen profession, we'd understood a long time ago that every moment of ours was borrowed time, and so we'd had more than one conversation about what would come next. We both agreed a time to grieve was necessary, but the one thing Tony had taught me was how not to get lost in your grief. The days after Zion had been murdered were the hardest of my life because I truly hadn't wanted to go on. So much of me had died with him, I'd literally wanted to die too, and had it not been for Tony, I surely would have. Now that it was my brother, my life coach and best friend, I didn't know how not to drown in this pool of grief, but I knew I had to figure the shit out quickly. I took a few deep breaths as I wrapped the towel around my body, and then I opened the bathroom door.

"Do I even want to know how long you've been standing here waiting for me?" I asked, looking deep into Mo's dark brown eyes.

"I'm worried about you. I haven't seen you like this since…"

"Since my husband was killed. Trust me when I tell you this shit hurts the same way, but I know I've gotta keep myself in check, because I promised Tony I would if it ever came to this," I said, moving past her and sitting down on the queen-sized bed in her spare bedroom.

"You know he would do the same if it was you. It would be just as hard, but he'd hold it together if for no other reason than little Zion."

"Yeah, I know," I replied softly.

I sat there, looking down at my hands until I saw tears appear in my palms, and run through the cracks in my fingers. The ache in my chest was so real that I couldn't put it into words, but I knew I was forever broken now. I didn't fight Mo when she went into the bathroom and came out with some lotion, then kneeled in front of me and began to apply it to my legs.

"Thank you," I said, laying back on the bed and staring at the ceiling.

Her soft hands worked like magic as she massaged the lotion into my legs, and I allowed my mind to drift far away from the chokehold Tony's loss caused. It wasn't until she got to the inner part of my thighs that I realized my pussy was wet and throbbing with need. I'd been in sexually tense situations before with her, so I knew there was a natural attraction, but I'd never acted on it or allowed her to. For that reason alone, I knew it surprised the shit out of her when I opened my legs a little wider. She didn't miss a beat though, she just kept on applying the lotion with an expert sensuality that gave me goosebumps.

"Turn over," she demanded softly.

I moved to do what she wanted, and before I knew it, I found myself face down on her bed, without my towel or any other piece of clothing to cover me. I felt her hands on me first, massaging, searching, and releasing the built-up frustrations, but then everything changed when her tongue joined the party. The way she licked my inner thigh while her hands grabbed both of my ass cheeks and spread them apart, pushed an involuntary moan from my throat. I had two fistfuls of her silk sheets by the time she moved her tongue from one thigh to the other, and higher up to my sweet spot.

"Ohhh," I panted when she took her first lick of me.

Her grip on my ass was firm so I couldn't run from her, but it was gentle at the same time. The way the tip of her tongue shadowboxed with my clit, made my toes crack involuntarily and my back arch in surrender, but it wasn't enough.

"M-make me c-cum," I demanded.

"Oh, I will, just hold on tight."

I thought she was being funny, but within the next few seconds of her licking my clit and sucking on my pussy lips, I had to double down on my grip. I fought the screams that were threatening to rattle my vocal cords, but that was the only fight I was winning, because the fight for my body was lost. The moment I felt the quivering start in my toes I knew what was coming. Me!

"Mo-Mo-Mo," I chanted, writhing back and forth as the pressure continued to build rapidly.

I felt her slide two of her fingers inside me, and the amount of force used was just enough to ring my bell of fulfillment. I came hurricane hard and lightning quick, and it didn't stop after the first wave. In the middle of my climax, she roughly flipped me back over and dove headfirst into my pussy, like it was hers to have forever. When her lips locked around my clit and she started sucking while humming, I grabbed her by two handfuls of her blonde hair, and I held on like my life depended on it. My legs locked around her head on their own, and the way my cum was gushing out of me made me fearful that I might drown her. Normally my climax subsided quickly after reaching the second peak, but when she started flicking her tongue rapidly back and forth across my clit again, I discovered a new level of ecstasy.

"Ho-holllyyyy shitttttt!" I cried out, filled with shock and awe.

Mo drank from me like I was the Holy Grail containing the last remaining drops of Jesus's blood, and this was the only way to get saved. All I could do was hang on and that's exactly what I did, until the shaking finally subsided. Even in the shadows, I could see the self-satisfied grin on her face as she backed away from me, but I was too weak to do anything about it.

"Th-thanks," I said weakly.

"You're more than welcome, and it was my pleasure. It's late, so why don't you get some sleep and we'll talk in the morning."

"I can't, I left Zion at home with his little friend and—"

"And he'll be fine because you have good people around him. You're not in any condition to be around him tonight anyway, and you know that."

I wanted to argue some more, but I knew it was useless because Mo was the most logical person I knew. So, I saved my breath, and motioned for her to lay down in the bed beside me instead. She came to me, and we spooned like we had in the past when we'd fallen asleep in the same bed together. When sleep claimed me a short time later, it was from sheer exhaustion, but I was grateful, nonetheless. Of course, my sleep was plagued with dreams, and these dreams were beautiful nightmares because I was spending time with Tony and Zion. I could feel the love for both of them swell inside me, but I knew even in my dream that the pain was just around the corner. I'd dreamed of Zion before, and no matter how it turned out, I always loved them because I felt like it was him crossing through time and space to be with me once again. This dream was different though. Somehow, I could sense he was worried, and instead of trying to hold me and talk to me, he was yelling at me. When I looked towards Tony, I saw he was mimicking Zion's actions, and this caused a feeling inside me that I couldn't describe. I wanted desperately to know what the hell they were screaming at me, but it was like watching two mimes go through their routine because there was no sound.

"Snow…Snow, it's ok," Mo said, holding me tighter.

When I opened my eyes, I was surprised to find her face-to-face with me, only a breath away.

"Uh, why are you this close when you know your morning breath is fierce?" I asked, smiling.

I'd expected some type of smartass retort, but her eyes were clouded with enough concern to make me look at her differently.

"What's wrong, Mo?"

"You were screaming and going crazy in your sleep, begging Zion and Tony to come back. I tried shaking you to wake you up, but nothing worked, so I climbed back in bed with you and held you until you could hear me."

Had she not been doing exactly what she described, I wouldn't have believed what she was saying, but her arms around me, coupled with the look on her face, said it all.

"I'm good, really. I was dreaming about both of them and they were yelling at me, but I couldn't hear them."

"Did they look concerned?" she asked, genuinely curious.

I knew dream interpretation was something of a hobby with her, so I knew this question was one of many to follow. I'd known Mo since high school, and the best way to describe her would be to say that she was eccentric in the best possible way. She was loyal as fuck though, and that quality was the one I'd always admired the most, because I needed no fuck niggas or bitches around me.

"I'm thinking on the same wavelength you are, so to answer your main question, yes, I think they're trying to warn me," I replied.

"Both men knew you, and since I know you, I know you're probably gonna go at Campa for what he did. Do I need to tell you why that's a bad idea?"

"No, you don't and no, that's actually not my move right now. I still have a question about why somebody would set Tony up like that, because I know damn well he didn't steal something as small as a ton of coke. I need to know who, what, when, and why because whoever set him up has to view me as an enemy too," I said.

"Not necessarily. I mean, it could be someone trying to move up into Tony's spot as your right-hand, or as Campa's right-hand. You know like I do Tony was in a prime spot regardless of who the boss is, and it would've only taken death to replace him."

"That's what makes this shit so crazy!" I said, blowing out a breath in frustration as I untangled our limbs, and sat up in the bed. "Campa should've never gone for this bullshit...so why did he?" I questioned aloud.

"Maybe Campa just stopped trusting Tony, and he was waiting for a reason to take him out."

"He's El Jefe of this organization, which means he don't need a fucking excuse to kill someone under his command," I said.

"True...but if he just kills Tony outright for no reason, he knows he's gonna rip his organization in half, because you're not hearing nothing after that. Having a reason, even a flimsy one like this one, is still better than having no reason, and it keeps you in the fold."

"But why, Mo? What did Tony do to Campa?"

"I honestly don't know, bae, but have you ever thought about how close you and Tony were? Once upon a time that was Campa's right-hand man and most trusted advisor, which made him next in line for the throne. But Tony didn't choose to pursue that future, he instead chose to be everything you and Zion Junior needed, and in the process, he alienated the one person who'd put him on. Do you think that didn't hurt Campa's feelings...because even murdering sociopaths have feelings," she replied.

I opened my mouth to shoot a thousand holes in her theory, but I found myself with my mouth hanging open without a word to speak. There was a twisted logic to what Mo was saying, and it made me sick to my stomach to acknowledge that. I'd known Campa for years, so I knew just how ruthless he was, but I'd never looked at him as someone who was insecure enough to do the things he'd done, for the reason Mo had described. The problem was, it wasn't out of the realm of possibilities and that meant eventually, him and I would have to butt heads like rams on the side of a mountain. I couldn't let him know that though, because he wouldn't hesitate to kill me, my son, and anyone else close to me.

"I need to ask something of you, Mo, and you can say no if you need to because it's dangerous as shit."

"Danger makes everything more fun, doesn't it?"

"I'm serious, Mo. This shit can go sideways really quick, and I don't want anything to happen to you."

"I hear you, Snow, so what do you need?"

"I need you to be my right-hand and pick up where Tony left off. That's the only way I'll be able to look into what happened with Tony, without worrying about business suffering, or Campa catching wind of what I'm doing. I've gotta move in silence, and I need you to be my unseen hand. In order for that to work though, we can't let what just happened distract us, and we have to keep it between us so no one can exploit it as a weakness. We also have to grow eyes in the back of our heads because if Campa, or whoever is behind Tony's setup, views you as a threat then they'll come for you too. I can't lose you too, Mo."

"You won't lose me, and you don't have to ask me twice. I'll ride with you into hell and overthrow the devil from his throne, smiling the whole time."

Aryanna

Chapter 10

One week later

"Mom, I don't wanna go."

"I know sweetheart, and I wish we didn't have to go, but paying your respects is the only way to truly say goodbye and have some type of closure," I said softly.

"I don't wanna say goodbye."

The look of devastation on my son's face tore at my heart, the same way it had been ever since I'd worked up the courage to tell him his godfather and hero was gone. In the last week, I'd barely seen Junior, even though I'd tried to grieve with him by taking off work and keeping him home from school. He locked himself in his room for the most part, only coming out when I forced him to join me for a meal. I'd known it was beyond painful when he'd refused each and every visit from Alexia, and her phone calls too. I hated to see my little man in pain, but there was no way around it, only through it.

"Come here, baby," I said, taking a seat on my bed and patting the spot next to me so he'd come sit with me.

Despite how handsome he looked in his black Gucci suit, I could see he was fighting valiantly not to cry. He'd broken down in front of me a time or two, but for the most part, I heard him sniffling when I was standing on the other side of his bedroom door.

"Baby boy, I know how bad this hurts you because I'm going through it with you, and I'd give anything to not be. I miss Tony more than I can put into words, and I really don't want to see him in a coffin, but I don't wanna regret it either."

"I won't regret it, Mom...honestly, I just want to keep the last memories I have of my uncle Tony the way they were. We had fun on my birthday while you were working, and I want to remember him like that, not in some wood box. The Tony I knew was too big for that box, and I don't wanna see him like that," he said softly.

The point my nine-year-old made to me demonstrated the wisdom that surpassed his years, and it put tears in my eyes as my heart beat a little harder. How did I argue with what he was saying? There was no argument to be had, and I truthfully didn't want one because I wanted him to know I could and would respect his feelings.

"I never thought about it like that, Zion, but you're absolutely entitled to miss the service if that's what you want to do. You need to be sure though."

"I've thought about it a lot, Mom…it's all I've thought about. I know Tony would understand because we had a special relationship like that. Please don't make me go, Mom," he said, looking over at me with tears streaming silently down his face.

The pain in his eyes was too much for me, and I pulled him to me. I held him tight and let him cry until he was all cried out for the moment. I knew there were no words that would take this pain away, so I offered up no hollow platitudes. Instead, I gave my son the love I knew his father and uncle would want for him, while silently praying for them to watch over him and help heal the hole in his heart. We stayed locked in that same embrace until Mo appeared in the doorway and gave me a knowing look. The form-fitting black dress hugged everything on her that no one could see, but today wasn't about her sex appeal or the situationship we'd found ourselves in since that fateful night. Right now, her presence served to steady me, because I needed to be stronger than I'd ever been for Junior, and myself.

"You don't have to go, Junior, but I do, so are you okay staying home by yourself?" I asked, pulling back so I could look down at him.

He looked so much younger than his actual age as he nodded his head, while wiping the tears from his face with the back of his hand.

"He's not going?" Mo asked from the door.

I shook my head at her, and she left it at that.

"I want you to eat something, Junior, and then lay down for a little while, okay?" I suggested gently.

"Yes ma'am," he replied softly.

I dropped a quick kiss on his forehead before moving past him and heading out the room. When I got to the door, I turned back to see if he was following me, but he had already kicked off his shoes and climbed up into my bed. Ordinarily, I would've told him to go get in his own bed, but my instincts told me he wanted to be close to me while I was gone, so I left it alone.

"Is he okay?" Mo asked, once we'd made our way downstairs.

"I honestly don't know, but I respect his reasoning for not wanting to go to the service. He's hurting and it's killing me to see him go through this. I never wanted him to know this type of pain again."

"Of course, you didn't. It kinda makes you think about what would happen if he lost you, huh?" she asked.

I couldn't even put into words the amount of fear that had suddenly developed inside me over the past seven days at that very thought, but I knew it wasn't something that I could give into. This wasn't the movies, where there was some type of retirement plan for the kingpin in the end, and I knew that. I was in it, and I was in it to win it, all because there was no other way.

"You drive," I said, passing her the keys to my truck, while leading the way out of the house.

As soon as I hopped in the passenger seat, I started going through the routine check of my guns, making sure everything was where it was supposed to be. In honor of Tony, I'd bought a new AK-74 (Draco) with the hundred-round drum full of hollow points, and I kept that bitch in my lap like my newborn baby. It took us a little more than half an hour to make it to the church Tony's family had chosen for the service, and I wasn't surprised to see the parking lot full to compacity for attendance.

"He was loved," I said softly.

"That he was, that he was. We don't have to do this though, Snow, and you know he would understand."

"Yeah, he would, but I know he'd do it for me. Let's go," I said, concealing the Draco inside my oversized purse, and getting out.

The moment my stilettos hit the pavement, I made sure to hold my head high and straighten my spine, because I knew I walked with the spirit of two kings resting on my shoulder.

"I need you to remain calm and remember you're all Zion Junior has right now," Mo said, walking up on me and blocking me from moving towards the church.

I started to ask her why she felt the need to reiterate what was already understood, but I suddenly spotted someone over her shoulder who shouldn't have been here.

"You two look lovely, and I'm sure Tony is smiling down from heaven right now."

"Th-thank you Jefe," I replied, fighting with all my might to keep my voice neutral, and not infuse the rage that I felt.

The balls on this motherfucker left me astounded, but I knew that he wanted to catch me off guard, so I kept it real cute.

"You look handsome yourself, but when don't you dress to impress?" I asked casually.

"Too true. Normally, I wear white, but for this somber occasion I felt traditional black was appropriate. Where is little Zion?" he asked, looking towards the rear of my truck.

"He wasn't feeling up to it, so I allowed him to miss the service. He's taking this loss very hard," I replied.

"Understandable. He's young and strong-minded though, so I'm sure he will become immune to death like all of us have. That will make him stronger, no?"

The way he asked this question made me involuntarily clench my purse to me tighter, but a quick look at Mo told me that it wasn't smart to do what I was thinking. No matter how badly he was asking for it.

"You're right, Jefe, but we adults understand in a way that a child can't, so I must allow him to grow and develop at his own rate. I'll tell him you asked about him though," I said calmly.

"Ah."

His reply was short, but I could've sworn his eyes were smiling at me. It became perfectly clear to me in this moment that whether he'd killed Tony for a real or make-believe reason didn't matter, because he wasn't sorry either way. In his mind, Tony had outlived his usefulness, so he was simply resetting the balance of power. Maybe he'd felt Tony and I together was a threat to his throne, and so he had to eliminate that threat. I didn't know for sure, but the longer I shared the same air with him, the more I became convinced this was the truth.

"Will you need time off the way you did when Zion died?" he asked.

"No, Jefe, there's too much work to be done to take days off," I replied.

"It's good that you know this. I'll see you both inside."

My feet stayed rooted in their spot until he'd made it up the church steps and disappeared inside, and then I turned to Mo.

"Am I trippin?" I asked.

"No, he's definitely baiting you to see how you react, and you did the absolute right thing by not falling into any of it."

"I'm getting a bad feeling, Mo, because that man knows I ain't nothing to fuck with…so why is he doing it?"

"I don't know, but we need to find out the answer to that question fast because—"

The way she abruptly stopped talking had me reaching inside my purse as my eyes followed hers. When I saw what had her stuck, I let my hand drop further inside my purse until I had the Draco in my grip.

"What the fuck are you doing here, Phillisa?" I asked aggressively.

"I'm just trying to pay my respects to an old friend."

"You two weren't friends, I asked him that after we had our little lunch date last week, so try again. I advise you to tell the truth this time though, or the next funeral you go to will be your own," I stated, pulling my gun out.

"I mean you no disrespect and no harm, but if you raise that gun at me, your brains will go all over your friend here. You know me, and if you've done your homework then you know I'm plugged in to all the right places. When we first met, I wasn't myself, so what would make you think that I would be now?" she asked calmly.

Immediately my eyes started scanning our surroundings, but I didn't see anything out of place. Of course, that meant absolutely nothing because like Phillisa had said, I'd done my homework on her.

"They may get me, but I'll definitely get you, so you need to decide if this is worth you dying for," I said.

"I'm nothing if not loyal, so if I die paying my respects to my friend, then so be it. It was meant to be," she replied, walking past me and on into the church.

I looked to Mo with the question of what the hell I was supposed to do next, and the look she gave me said she was confused, but down for whatever. I knew Tony wouldn't want me to turn this into a shit show out here in public, so I put the gun away and gave Mo the nod to follow me inside. The service lasted for two hours, and I spent the majority of the time watching Phillisa. The crazy thing was that I wasn't the only one watching her, because Campa had his eyes glued to her every movement. When the service was over, everyone filed out the church, but Phillisa stayed seated in her pew staring at the coffin. When it was only me, her, and Mo left in the church, I passed Mo my purse, and I went and sat beside her in the pew. Neither of us spoke for a few moments, but it didn't feel as tense as our encounter outside.

"I asked Tony if he knew you, and he acted like he didn't. Why would he do that if you two were friends, Phillisa?"

"It's complicated."

"Can you understand why I'm gonna need you to uncomplicate it for me rather quickly? We're sitting here after just attending the funeral of one of the only family members I had left in this world, and I know for a fact he shouldn't be in that coffin. I also know he was set up. Given the fact that you work for my competitor I'm sure that you can understand my distrust of you right now," I said.

"I do understand, just like I understand that my connection to Zion is what's warring with what you think are your instincts telling you to distrust me. So, I guess it's more than complicated, but I get it. I'm not your enemy, Claudette, and

95

you know that because if you thought otherwise, then one of us would be dead by now."

"It's still early in the day, so don't speak too soon," I replied seriously.

The smile that lit up her face as she turned towards me, seemed completely out of place in this environment and situation, but it was radiant, nonetheless. In order to survive in this world, I'd had to learn how to read people in an instant, and from the very beginning, I'd known Phillisa had secrets. I just hadn't gotten the feeling that her secrets could hurt me. My instincts hadn't changed about that, but my quest for the truth spurred me on when it came to searching for her hidden agenda.

"Who are you, Phillisa?" I asked.

"The answer to that question is even more complicated than the answer to why Tony would act like he didn't know me. Are you sure you wanna know though?"

For some reason, my brain started tingling when she asked that question, but the challenge swimming in her eyes made turning back impossible at this point.

"Who are you?" I asked again.

"My name is Phillisa…and Campa is my father."

Chapter 11

I knew my mouth was literally hanging at full tilt because my jaw hurt, and I could taste the flowery fragrance riding on the air. Without a doubt, I knew I'd misheard her though.

"Um, I'm sorry, can you repeat that?" I asked slowly.

"I said, I'm Campa's daughter. I'm sure he doesn't talk about me, and has probably never mentioned me, but that won't make me disappear. Much to his annoyance."

"You're full of shit," I blurted out, shaking my head.

"Oh, trust me, we did the whole DNA thing when I was still an infant, and I'm one hundred percent his bastard child."

The way she spoke about it held no bitterness, but her eyes clouded over with a pain that needed no words to interpret.

"If you're telling the truth, then this shit is beyond complicated, but it doesn't explain why Tony would deny knowing you," I said, getting back to the subject of importance.

"Doesn't it though? If Tony would've told you who I was, would you not have had a million questions that needed answering? If I know Tony, he was more concerned with why I was back in Miami than having to answer all of those questions."

"Back in Miami? So, you really are from here? Why did you leave?" I asked curiously.

"That's a long story, and it involves my father. Let me sum it up by saying he's an uncompromising man, even when it comes to his own child, and so it was either leave or die."

"Die? I know Campa is coldblooded, but he'd never hurt his own flesh and blood," I stated.

For a moment she simply stared at me without speaking, and then she gave me the saddest smile I'd ever seen.

"Claudette, I'm sure you think you know who my father is, and I'm sure you've seen him at his most ruthless, but I promise you that you have no clue who he is or what he's capable of. If you know like I do, you'll remember that…or pick out what you wanna be buried in," she said, turning to face Tony's coffin again.

I knew I hadn't mentioned the fact that Campa had killed Tony, but I got the strange feeling Phillisa somehow knew that truth. It made me wonder what else she knew, and how she knew it.

"So, if you left because your dad was gonna kill you, then why have you returned? Given the way he was watching you, I'd take a guess and say you two still aren't on the best of terms, and I'll tell you now that he's as deadly as ever."

"I don't doubt it. To answer your question though, I'm back because I'm tired of running. I've learned to fear no man, not even El Diablo himself, so I'm back and I brought a surprise with me."

"A surprise? Oh yeah, what's that?" I asked.

"Power."

At first, I didn't understand her response, but then I thought about what I'd learned when I'd done my homework on her father.

"How did you manage to do that though? I mean somewhere down the drug pipeline your two paths have to cross, and that can make shit ugly," I said.

"True, but money is power, and he or she who makes the money has the power. Let's just say I make a lot of money, and not even the all-powerful Campa can stop that."

I wanted to question whether or not she was telling the truth, but I knew if she was actually who she said she was, and they actually had a problem, then money would be the only thing that could change the tide.

"You didn't answer my question, Phillisa…why are you back, because just being homesick is not enough to make you risk your life."

You want the truth?" she asked, turning back to me, and moving closer so that we couldn't be overheard.

"Of course, I want the truth."

"I had to come back. I owe my father something, and I've come to give it to him," she replied.

"Enough with the cryptic shit, bitch, just tell me what the play is."

The fact that she laughed at my impatience only frustrated me more, but I resisted the urge to smack the lip gloss off her mouth. She could see my anger building though, and she immediately held up her hand in surrender.

"I promise, all of your questions will be answered in due time, but for now I just need you to get me from under this bogus indictment," she said.

"From where I'm sitting, I can't tell it's bogus, so…"

"Oh, it's bogus, and I know my father is behind it," she said calmly.

"Wait-what?"

"I said, my father is behind it. He can't kill me now, so his only move is to get me thrown beneath the jail for all of eternity."

"Damn, does he really hate you that much?" I asked.

Again, her response was to laugh lightly and shake her head at my naivety.

"Campa loves nothing and no one, what the hell did you do to make him feel this way?" I asked.

For a split second, her eyes were unguarded, and she gave me a look of guilt I didn't understand. Before I knew it though she'd tucked it away, and her poker face was back intact, protecting her secrets from the world at large.

"I didn't do anything women haven't been doing since the dawn of time. I won't apologize for it and if I have to, I'll die for it. That's all you need to know."

I could tell by the set of her jaw that she was done talking, so there was no need to try and beat the truth out of her.

"Look, I ain't trying to be in the middle of whatever this bullshit is, so I think you should get a new lawyer because—"

"You're already in the middle of it," she said.

"How do you figure that?"

"Who killed Tony?" she asked nonchalantly.

The look on her face said I didn't need to speak the answer out loud, because we both knew the truth. The only thing I was really wondering was how the hell she knew the truth without a hinting of doubt.

"Tony's death doesn't put me in the middle of this shit with Campa and you."

"It does, because you care about Tony, and I know that because you were just ready to shoot me out front to keep the memory of him all to yourself. That's love in any language, and for that kind of love, you'll burn the world and all things in it," she stated confidently.

Instead of replying to her statement, I turned my eyes towards the casket still sitting at the front of the empty church. Even though my body was here in this very real moment, my heart and mind were in another real moment that was taking place in my own heart. It wasn't just my love for Tony that I had to consider, I had to factor in Junior's love too. No one was allowed to harm my child without there being serious repercussions, which meant Phillisa was right. I was in this now.

"Since you know or believe your charges are bogus, maybe you can tell me how I'm supposed to get around them," I said.

"That's where you earn your money, Mrs. Snow. I know there's a reason you're the baddest bitch when it comes to that law shit in this part of the world, so I'm not worried."

"Good to know I have your confidence," I replied sarcastically.

She chuckled softly, but she nodded her head in the affirmative.

"I have all the confidence in you and if I didn't, then I surely would've taken my business elsewhere. I didn't pick you because you're the closest person to my father."

"Am I really supposed to believe that?" I asked.

"It doesn't matter if you believe it or not, because it's the truth regardless. I had no intentions on telling you the sordid history of my family, and I also had no reason to target you. You and I have more in common than you know, so if anything, I considered the potential of you as an ally and not an enemy. I wouldn't put my life in my enemy's hands."

Her statement was too logical not to be true, but I knew it would be smart of me to sleep with one eye open when it came to her and this situation. None of us were girl scouts, and all parties had blood on their hands for sure.

"I hear you, and I will do what I can to get you acquitted. In the meantime, I suggest you lay low and stay away from dear old dad," I said.

"I won't make you any promises I can't keep. With that being said though, I promise you the things my father has done will not go answered for."

The instant fire in her eyes suddenly confirmed any doubts I had about her actually being Campa's long lost daughter. In this moment, she looked just like him, but I wasn't about to say that.

"Why don't you visit with Tony for a while longer? I need to go check on my son and make sure he's okay, because he's taking this loss harder than ever."

"I understand only too well. You go, and I'll contact you at another time, but do me a favor though?" she asked.

"What do you need?"

"Keep your eyes open, and make sure anyone close to you does the same," she replied, looking pointedly at Mo.

"I got you," I said, standing up to leave.

We exchanged a look that needed no words to translate it, and then I motioned to Mo that it was time for us to move on. As I walked outside, I contemplated every word spoken in the conversation between Phillisa and I, wondering how much wasn't being said, because there was a lot of truth revealed. I knew I couldn't trust her regardless, but I could give her the benefit of the doubt until it was no longer wise to do so.

"What was all that about?" Mo asked, once we were back in the truck.

"I'm not sure, but if she's telling even a portion of the truth, then it's about to be some shit out here in these streets."

"Well, don't be tight-lipped, bitch, fill me in," she demanded, starting my truck and pulling off.

As she navigated the roads back to my house, I ran down my entire conversation with Phillisa. Just hearing the words come out of my mouth gave me a different perspective on her as a person, because I was now evaluating everything from the moment we'd met up until now, with my newfound knowledge.

"So, how do you think we should play this?" Mo asked once we'd pulled up in front of my house.

I considered all the answers to that question, weighing out the pros and cons of each decision made. At the end of the day it was looking more and more like a war was unavoidable, and if that was the case then I need to be as prepared as possible.

"Let's go check on things," I said.

"You mean now? And where do you wanna go?"

"I wanna check on my entire operation from the ground level on up. I want you to call meetings with our biggest distributors, and make sure that you let them know that I want to see them in person instead of their allowed delegates. I want to make sure that everyone is on the same page," I replied.

"I understand, so where do you wanna start?"

I thought on that for a moment until the answer came to me like Tony was sitting in the truck with us.

"I wanna check on the work, so let's hit the stash houses before we start to meet with people," I suggested.

Mo nodded her head while putting my truck in reverse and backing out of the driveway. I had several stash houses around the city, but I changed the schedule by which the work was delivered and moved through them at least twice a week. I already knew the consequences for becoming predictable out here in these streets. While we rode from spot to spot taking inventory on the product and the money, I started amassing a list of the people who currently worked for me. After two and a half hours of riding around, I picked up my phone and summoned a total of ten people to meet me at a secret location.

"What are you about to do?" Mo asked curiously.

"Make sure my employees remain loyal to me. Come on."

I got out of the truck and led the way into the two-story house I owned under a fake identity. Getting involved in real estate had been my way of paying homage to Zion, but in reality, it served many purposes. Sometimes, there were situations like this that came up, and I needed somewhere to handle business without the prying eyes of normal society. When we

walked through the door my street lieutenant, Silk, was waiting for us in the foyer.

"Everybody here?" I asked.

"Yeah, they're all in the living room, sipping some twelve-
hundred-dollar a bottle Cognac, discussing profits from last
quarter," he replied.

"Good job, Silk, remind me to give you a raise when this
is over," I said.

"I can take care of that," Mo offered, smiling devilishly.

"Bring your ass, bitch," I said, leading the way into the
living room.

"Gentlemen, I appreciate all of you coming out on such
short notice, and I promise I won't hold you up too long," I
said, holding my hand out to accept my purse from Mo.

"What's all of this about, Snow? Campa never mentioned
a meeting in the middle of the month," Alberto said.

"I'm glad you asked, Alberto, because what you said has
everything to do with why we're here. All of you work for me,
but you've had some direct dealings with Campa or you came
from his organization. At this point in time, I'm sorry to say,
but I'm forced to question your loyalty," I stated, pulling the
Draco from my purse.

There were looks of surprise on a few of the faces surrounding me, but for the most part, everyone remained un-
fazed. These weren't men that scared easily, nor would they
beg for their lives in the face of death. I liked that about them,
but sadly it wasn't enough of a reason to spare their lives.
Without another word, I levelled the gun at the man closest to
me, and I let that bitch breathe.

Chapter 12

One month later

"All rise! The Honorable Judge Maurice Terry presiding!"

"You may be seated," the judge said, taking his seat behind the bench.

I'd spent enough time in courtrooms to know how to read both the judge and the jury, and the vibe I was getting right now caused me to smile slightly.

"I've reached my decision in the matter of the United States versus Phillisa Toreno. Based on the evidence presented by the state, I find that I have to side with counsel for Ms. Toreno and say that there's not enough here to bring this case to trial. The burden of proof needed to point the finger at Ms. Toreno as the mastermind behind the drug bust that occurred at the address listed in this indictment has not been met. Therefore, it is the ruling of this court that all charges against Ms. Toreno be dismissed accordingly. Ms. Toreno, you're free to go."

The bang of the gavel proceeded the applause that thundered through the courtroom from those here to support Phillisa. Ordinarily, I wouldn't have called for character witnesses to fill the galley before the trial was even set, but Phillisa was a business woman with ties to the local community, as well as ties to the Hispanic community at large in the surrounding cities of Florida. Calling her a drug dealer was like calling Barack Obama an immigrant that wasn't born here, or at least that's the picture I'd painted for everyone. When I'd attended law school, one of the first things I'd learned was that the law came down to who the best storyteller was. Whoever could sell it the best was the one whose hand would be lifted in victory at the end, and today that was me.

"Nice job, Mrs. Snow. Dinner is on me tonight," Phillisa said, smiling widely.

"You know where to meet me," I replied, quickly packing up my briefcase.

I accepted the congratulations of those around me, but I really wasn't interested in the praise. For me, this was just a chess move in the game of life, but it didn't hurt my defense record or reputation to get another win. While everyone was preoccupied with Phillisa, I grabbed my stuff and slipped out of the side door that led downstairs to the underground garage. As soon as I came out of the stairway into the garage, I spotted Campa's silver Cadillac Escalade parked beside my Aston Martin. My steps didn't falter in the slightest, because in all actuality I'd known this moment was coming, and I was prepared for it. I didn't go to my car and try to act like I didn't know who he was or why he was here, I went straight to the rear passenger door, opened it and climbed in.

"Are you here to take me to a celebratory dinner, because if you are, I'm sorry to tell you I've already made plans."

"Why didn't you do like I told you and lose that case, Claudette?"

"Do like you told me?" I repeated slowly, turning in my seat to look at him.

He didn't look at me directly, but instead continued to look straight ahead while calmly stroking the Glock .45 sitting in his lap.

"Have you forgotten who you work for, Claudette? Have you forgotten who made you?" he asked softly, yet forcefully.

I could feel the heat rising from my neck and travelling up to my face as his words sunk into my brain. I knew he was doing more than baiting me now, and the fact that I wasn't afraid in this moment told me I needed to tread lightly.

"I haven't forgotten anything, Campa, including the mutually beneficial business arraignment we've had over the past five years. As to why I didn't lose the case load for my entire career, and I think you know why that's a bad idea. It wouldn't have stopped there, because you know the district attorney would've absolutely looked over my cases. So, with all due respect, Campa, I suggest you let me handle the legal matters while you handle the illegal empire that you've built. Right now, I work with you, but at the rate you're going, I'll be representing you in a court of law soon."

I could tell by the way he was clenching his jaw that he had a real problem with what I was saying, but he couldn't argue with the truth. I gave him a few seconds to try and refute what I was saying though, and when no words came from his mouth, I opened the truck's door and climbed out. Without a backwards glance, I hopped in my car, started the engine and pulled off. The smile on my face probably would've gotten me shot if Canpa could've seen it, but his ignorant ass was still sitting in the garage, trying to figure out how to outmaneuver his own child. I would've felt bad for him had I not known his heartless ass probably deserved whatever came next. The only thing I knew was it was becoming more and more evident that there would be some type of showdown between Campa and me, and it was liable to happen sooner than later. Mo-Mo and I had discussed that very real possibility this morning when I told her it was almost a certainty, I would get Phillisa off. I knew Campa would be mad, I just didn't know how he would react. When I pulled up at the traffic light, I dug my phone out of my pocket, with the intention of calling Mo so I could let her know what happened. I'd just punched in the last digit when an all-white panel van slid to a stop alongside the driver's side of my car, and the doors swung open. I'd seen enough BET movies for my instincts to kick in, and before it became a conscious thought, I'd dropped my phone so I could grab my pistol. Suddenly, a masked face appeared at my window, and his hand was reaching for the driver's side door handle. I knew he probably thought he was one step closer to victory when my door opened, but it was short-lived because my first shot sprayed his brains all over the side of the van. The hesitation by the dead man's partner, gave me the option to close my door and pull off, but I chose to do what they wouldn't expect by putting my car in park. With my gun outstretched in my hand, I swiftly stepped out of my car, took quick aim at the now retreating man in all-black, and fired three more shots. His head exploded with the same finality as the first man's and that made me smile inside. I had no idea how many people were left in the van, but I took advantage of the side door being open by emptying my clip at the figure in the driver's seat. I heard the rev of the van's engine, signaling its intent to pull off, but by the time my gun clicked to signify it being empty, the van had returned to a normal idle and it wasn't moving. I slid back into the safety of my car, closed the door, and reached for my back-up gun while searching blindly for my phone. Even though I didn't see anything else I perceived to be an immediate threat, I still kept my eyes on a swivel. When I finally felt my phone, I looked at it long enough to press send to connect my call to Mo, and then I put it on speaker phone so I could continue evaluating my situation.

"Hey, bae, I was just about to call you and—"

"Mo, I need you to listen to me real quick. Somebody just tried to either kill me or kidnap me. I knocked off at least three of them, but I have no idea how many more there are, and I'm still out here in traffic."

"Where the hell are you, Snow?" she asked, immediately panicked.

"I'm right down the street from the courthouse, which means the cops will be here within minutes. I need you down here ASAP, Mo."

"I'm coming," she said, hanging up in my ear.

I was about to call the cops and make my official report when I caught sight of another van approaching the intersection from the opposite direction. I probably wouldn't have paid attention to it had it not been for the fact that it was moving at an abnormal speed. It could've been the fact that there were bodies laying in the street, and whoever was behind the wheel was simply approaching with caution. That wasn't the feel I got though, and now wasn't the time to question what my gut was telling me. With my eyes still on the van coming towards me, I slid my car back into gear, and eased off from the light. I'd only made it about two feet before the van sped up and swerved in front of me to block my path. The side door swung open and all I saw was the rotating barrel of a 30mm machine gun winking at me. I immediately hit the brakes and threw the car in reverse. Despite having my shit armored to withstand this exact kind of attack, I wasn't so sure the alterations I'd made would stand up to that kind of firepower. Before I could swing a full U-turn and get gone with the wind, Campa's Escalade materialized out of nowhere, and slid to a stop between me and the other van. To say I was surprised was an understatement, but it couldn't have happened a moment too soon, because there was a sudden roar, and then Campa's truck was rocking on its springs. The back passenger door opened up, and Campa calmly stepped out like he didn't just jump into the middle of a gunfight. I threw my car back in drive and pulled right up on him so I could get out with him.

"Friends of yours?" I hollered over the gunfire.

"This is too messy for my tastes. Besides, you're familia," he replied, pulling his Glock .45 from his shoulder holster.

I nodded my thanks while checking the drum on my Draco to make sure I was locked and loaded. He did the same thing, and then we opened fire on the van from our vantage point behind his truck. I tried to take out whoever was operating the machine gun, but I couldn't get a clear shot nor could I see who it was. I wanted to run up on the van on some Tony Montana type shit, but this definitely wasn't the movies and I wasn't bulletproof.

"I can't get a clear shot," I yelled to Campa.

He nodded his understanding and I could see the frustration on his face, because he was suffering from the same problem.

"Cover me!" he yelled, diving into the backseat of his truck.

I stuck my gun up over the hood, and just kept my finger on the trigger. There was no way for me to aim, but the sounds of shells hitting the ground was harmonious and indicative that neither of us was out here playing. The sudden sound of sirens could be heard over the chorus of gunplay, but not even that was deterring whoever was behind this bold attempt on my life. When Campa slid back out of his truck, and I got a good look at what he was holding, I realized he didn't give a fuck about the cops coming either.

"You just ride around with that?" I asked, bewildered.

"Doesn't everyone?"

The smile lighting up his face was sinister but filled with joy all at the same time as he fitted the rocket to the RPG in his grip. His driver suddenly appeared with a rocket and RPG of his own, which made me feel like my poor little assault rifle was out of place. I kept firing though until both of them were loaded up, and then I took cover. The high-pitched screams sounded like something straight out of a video game, but the way the earth shook beneath my feet when the rockets met their targets spoke to just how real this was. When I peeked around Campa's Escalade, I was confused for a second, until I realized the hole in the asphalt was where the van used to be.

"Damn, Jefe," I said chuckling softly.

"Nobody fucks with la familia and lives to tell about it. Nobody except for the law that is, so with that said, I think it's time for me to make haste. Are you good?"

"Yeah, I'm good, you go and I'll meet you at your house when it's safe. Don't forget to call our people and have them alter these traffic cameras ASAP, so you were never here," I advised.

"Of course. Stay safe, my little snowbird."

Despite the situation and recent tension between Campa and me, I still smiled at his term of endearment, because it took me back to when I first started on this journey to become a queen of the dope game in my own right. The sound of the sirens getting closer staved off any further thoughts of going down memory lane though. Campa and his driver loaded up quickly and sped off in the opposite direction of the approaching calvary. It was less than a minute later when Morano's navy blue 2024 M6 BMW Coupe slid to a stop right behind my car, and she hopped out with her pistol at the ready.

"What the fuck happened?" she asked, taking in the carnage and destruction lining the streets.

"Well, obviously somebody is upset with me, but—"

"This ain't somebody, Snow, this is that bitch motherfucker, Campa! I'll kill him with my bare hands for this, I swear to—"

"It's not Campa, Mo, so calm down."

"What do you mean it's not Campa? I know you can't be that blind, Claudette! You think it's a coincidence that you and him ain't been on the same page, and you obviously chose his daughter's side in their little family squabble, and some hittas come after you? Come on, bae, you're way smarter than that shit you're talking."

"I'm not talking any shit, you are. I'm not saying Campa and me ain't been going through some shit, but this ain't on him, and I know this for a fact because he was just here banging it out with me. The crater over there is courtesy of the rocket launcher he keeps in his truck," I said, pointing to the scorch marks on the ground.

It was almost comical the way her eyes went from me to the spot I was pointing out and back to me. I read first disbelief, and then admiration in her eyes, but before we could discuss either, we were surrounded by Miami-Dade's finest.

"Put your guns down!" they yelled in unison.

"Move slowly, Mo," I said, bending down and putting my gun on the ground.

I made sure to put my hands straight up in the air after that, because I knew all too well how trigger happy the cops were.

"Morano, is that you?" a tall, dark-skinned man asked, coming from behind his open door.

"Hey Quan, long time no see," she replied.

"Everybody, lower your weapons, she works for the Department of Corrections, and her guns are all registered," Quan said, holstering his own weapon.

"Thanks, Q, I know this looks crazy, but it's all on the up and up," Mo said.

"Oh, I'm sure it is, so go ahead and start explaining."

Chapter 13

"I know it's late, and I dragged some of you away from your families at this time of night, but we're at war right now. I know by now you've all heard about the failed attempt to take me out today in downtown, but what you don't know is that we could be under attack from several different enemies."

"Who's at the top of the list, Snow?" Silk asked, continuing to wipe his chrome .40 Desert Eagle with the patience and attention reserved for a father and son.

"It could be a rival organization thinking we're weak because of some in-house tensions between me and Campa, but if I was to hazard a guess…I think it's the Columbians that are backing a client of mine."

Only Silk and Mo knew the name of the client, and right now that's the way I wanted it until I knew for sure what was going on. I didn't think Phillisa had started a war, I just had a feeling that part of her people's plan for her return involved taking over parts of Miami we currently controlled. It made logical sense, given the fact that she'd come back to take on her father, and Campa more or less owned damn near all of Florida. With my help, of course. So, there was no way the Columbians wouldn't back Phillisa's play against Campa, because at the end of the day, it was in furtherance of their main agenda. More money, more power.

"So, do we go after whoever you think it is, or do we wait until you're not so lucky and we're avenging your death?" Meatrock asked.

The sarcasm in his voice was caused by frustration and I understood it, because everyone on my team was like family. If you came for one, then you might as well come for all of us, because that's how we were carrying it. If I hadn't heard the annoyance in his voice, I definitely would've viewed it in the tight expression on his face.

"Meat, you know you're entirely too light-skinned to be balling your damn face up, so just chill out," I said smiling.

His expression didn't really change, but the wrinkles in his forehead relaxed a little. I couldn't be mad at him because it was his loyalty that made him act the way that he did. For him to be a young nigga, he moved like an old soul when it came to the streets and the politics used to govern them.

"To answer your question though, no, we're not moving on who I think is responsible. Never will I get too big to realize a worthy opponent when I see one, and no matter how many people we have behind us, the Columbians are still a force to be taken seriously. So, I'm gonna talk to my client, and find out what the situation is. For now, though, no one moves alone," I said, looking around my living room.

The people in this room were those I considered to be my inner circle and therefore, my most trusted. They were also the heart that beat when it came to keeping this thing moving and thriving, whether it be in the streets or in a business meeting. This was my team and I knew if a move had been made against me, then my team was next on somebody's list.

"Staying together is cool with me, but you know where I'll be," Meatrock said, looking down over his glasses at me.

"I got her, bruh, you good," Mo said.

Her voice was trying to project some nonchalance, but I viewed the protective look in her eyes, and I knew she was still seeing the scene from earlier.

"With all due respect, Morano, I'm moving by Snow's side until she tells me otherwise," Meat stated calmly.

"How about we decide this based on where I have to be, and when I have to be there. I say that because if I gotta be in court, then it makes sense for Mo to accompany me, and that way we have legal firearms on the premises. Meat, you know you're my nigga, but the big shit you carrying ain't legal in fifty out of fifty states."

His quick laughter signaled his surrender to the truth, and I breathed a sigh of relief at smoothly avoiding a pointless argument.

"Mo, you can tag along with me if you'd like," Silk offered, smiling.

The blush that heated up her face was instantaneous, and for some reason it irked the shit out of me.

"You ain't getting your dick wet right now, Silk, and you definitely ain't doing it with her, so pick another route," I stated in a matter of fact tone.

"My apologies, Jefa, I didn't realize that she was spoken for."

The sound of Jeezy snickering made me glance in his direction, but he was faking like he was too preoccupied with the blunt he was rolling to make eye contact with me.

"While you're laughing, Jeezy, I want you to make sure you put the word out on the street that everyone needs to keep their eyes open," I said.

"I got you, Snow, but you already know primetime stays ready," he replied smirking.

In today's climate, one needed more than one powerful ally to corner the streets in a way that spelled out dominance, so my alliance with the New York Brim Blood Army had been necessary. Jeezy was the current leader of the primetime set, and the team he commanded knew how to get money, as well as chop a motherfucker down when needed. Between him and Silk's team, I knew my street interests were well protected.

"What do you need me to do?" Ashlei asked.

"Starky, I want you to keep your eyes and ears open in your part of the world, because somehow the niggas on the inside seem to know when shit is gonna happen before we do," I replied.

She nodded her head in understanding, making sure to lock eyes with Mo. Ashlei Starky was another sergeant inside the Department of Corrections, and she worked with Mo to make shit happen behind the g-wall. When you were a sexy, five-foot-three-inch, one-hundred-fifty-pound, pigeon-toed redbone, the hardest of gangsters was putty in your hands, and Starky worked them niggas like no other. They would tell her shit that not even their mothers and baby mamas would know, and she was super stingy with the pussy, so all of this was done with the hopes that one day they would get to hit. I'd had the pussy already of course, and I knew for sure that if a nigga ever got ahold of some of that good shit, he'd kill at her command.

"Until further notice, I want everyone on scheduled check-ins via FaceTime," I said, looking around the room to make sure they knew I wasn't joking.

Once I was sure my point had been made, I turned towards Silk and gave him a nod.

"Alright, listen up. You all know we keep a special stockpile of weapons for wartime situations, and this definitely qualifies as that. I want all of you to go by the storage rooms, pick up some new hardware when you leave here, and put all of your personal guns away until this shit is dealt with. Take as much as you need, and make sure you get a vest too, because ain't none of you motherfuckers bulletproof," he said.

"What about Tony's family? Are we protecting them too?" Meat asked.

"You already know what it is, bruh. Tony was more than family to me, and I'll protect his people with my life, no matter what or who is coming after us," I replied seriously.

Everyone nodded their heads in agreement with how I was carrying it, but I hadn't expected anything different.

"I was just making sure, Snow. I got the first watch since Mo is here with you," Meat volunteered.

"That's fine. Just don't forget to call and check in on the regular, and when you leave from his house, I want you to come to my house," I said.

He nodded his head in agreement before standing up and heading towards the front door.

"What are you about to get into, Snow?" Silk asked.

"I need to go home and hold my son, because I almost lost the ability to do that today."

"I feel that. I'ma get rid of these bodies, and then I'm hitting the streets to see what's really poppin with niggas," he stated.

I knew just how crazy Silk was, underneath all that pretty boy shit, and I could tell by the look in his eyes that he felt some type of way about niggas trying to erase me from this earth.

"Be careful out there, Silk. I know how you feeling, trust me I know, but I need you to remain focused on the fact that this is a marathon and not a sprint. I need you to stay alive, my nigga," I said, staring at him intently.

The murderous intentions were in his eyes, and I knew he had to feed that animal before he could rest tonight.

"I'm good, Snow, that's my word."

"All a man has is his word," I stated as a reminder.

"True indeed," he replied, smiling at first me and then Morano.

To her credit, she kept a neutral expression on her face, but I knew her pussy was throbbing.

"Let's go, bitch," I said, pushing her towards the front door, and out into the cool night air.

"Let me find out that your ass is really jealous, Snow."

"Jealous? Of what? You know like I do, all it would take is an invitation for me to put this pussy on Starky's face for old time's sake," I said smiling.

"Probably, but we know her head game ain't better than mine."

I didn't say anything, but the huge grin stretching across my face said it all.

"You think this shit is a game, huh? I got something for that ass," Mo said, climbing into the passenger seat of my car.

I had no idea what she was talking about, but her fingers were tapping away at her phone's screen, and whatever message she was sending had her smiling wickedly. I paid her ass no mind as I started the car and pointed us in the direction of my primary residence. I hadn't made it to my house all day, despite my desire to hold Junior in my arms, so I was happy to finally be headed that way.

"Are you gonna stop and get something to eat on the way so we don't have to come back out?" she asked.

"Nah, I'll just order something from the restaurant to be delivered," I replied, pulling my own phone out.

It only took five minutes to order enough food to feed a small army, and I did that because I had no idea who would fall through my front door before the sun rose again. I couldn't help smiling at the thought of all the loyal motherfuckers I had willing to lay their lives down for me. It went without saying that I would do the same for any one of them, when and if the time came. It was how Zion would've done shit, so it was how I did shit. We pulled up to the house fifteen minutes later, and as soon as I came through the front door, Junior was flying into my arms.

"Mommy!"

"Hey, baby boy! I guess you missed me as much as I missed you, huh?"

"Yeah, I missed you, why didn't you come home after work today?" he asked, taking a step back so he could look up at me.

"I had a meeting to go to sweetie, I'm sorry. I ordered your favorite dishes from the restaurant to make up for not cooking dinner though. Will you eat with me?"

"I guess I can do that for you, but uh… Alexia is here, so is it okay if she stays for dinner too?" he asked, smiling bashfully.

Ordinarily, the pause of my heart in my chest would've been because my little man was growing up, and paying attention to girls more and more, but today was different. I paused when he asked me about Alexia, because I had to think like a parent right now. I knew being around me and mine wasn't the safest move for that little girl right now, and if I was her mom, I would want me to do the right thing by sending her home. On the other hand, though I had to think about Junior and what he needed. He'd lost someone who meant a lot to him, and unbeknownst to him, he had almost lost me too. So, was it not my responsibility as his mom to do what I could to make his life normal, if only for the night?

"I'm okay with Alexia staying, but you two have to stay in the house until it's time for her to go home, and I need to talk to her parents," I insisted.

"I know, Mom, I know."

The exasperation on his face was comical, and it was so much like his dad it hurt my heart, but I didn't let it show as I kissed his forehead.

"Come on," I said, putting my arm around his shoulders, and leading him further inside.

I looked over my shoulder to see Mo closing the door, while smiling at us and shaking her head. I took Junior into the kitchen where Alexia was waiting. I called her parents to make sure they were okay with her spending so much time over here, and then I got them situated with dinner. I made a plate and stayed with them for a little while just so I could steal a moment with Junior, but I could tell where his attention was. Since dinner was taken care of, I had a quick meeting with my security so they would know they were to shoot anyone who came on my property that wasn't approved or expected.

"I'm going upstairs to take a bath, Mo…are you coming?" I asked, giving her a knowing look.

"I'll be there in a minute, bae."

"I'll run the water," I said, smiling as I headed up the stairs.

The twinkle of naughty in Mo's eyes caused a tightness in my chest, but not in a bad way.

After going so long with only myself as a lover, it felt amazing to be able to let loose a little bit, especially because I didn't feel like Zion would've had a problem with what I was doing. Any time I'd been with a woman while he was alive, all he'd done was smile like a damn fool, and watch with his dick in his hand. To him, women were beautiful and meant to be appreciated, so he never minded me sharing myself with another woman. When I walked into my bedroom, I went straight to my master bathroom, and immediately filled the Jacuzzi tub up with hot water and scented oils. It wasn't until I started to undress myself that I realized I was crying silent tears. I stopped to evaluate what the fuck had me so emotional, and I instinctively knew it was Zion. Here I was, about to engage in some wild sexual shit with Mo-Mo, but my mind and heart were with my husband, and the fact that I'd almost reunited with him today only made me miss him more. My love for that man surpassed time and space, but it didn't come with pain, because it was a love of the purest form.

"I'll always love you, baby," I whispered, putting my hand over my heart to rub the tattoo with his name on it.

"Did you say something, Snow?" I turned around at the sound of Mo's voice, expecting to find her getting undressed, but I was greeted with another surprise.

"When did you get here, Ashlei?" I asked.

"A few moments ago. Mo hit me up and said that you wanted to put the band back together…or something of that nature."

I looked past Starky to Mo's devilish smile and stuck my middle finger up at her.

"Oh, you most definitely will fuck me, bae, because I'm not just here to watch you two. I wanna have fun, and you only live once."

Aryanna

Chapter 14

I undressed myself slowly, sensually, watching Starky and Mo staring at me with their mouths open and their hands unconsciously clenching into tight fists. I could feel their want riding the confined air of the bathroom, and it made my pussy wetter.

"Can one of you unhook this bra for me?" I asked, turning around slowly.

I quickly found out just how closely they were watching me because the moment I locked knees, and bounced my ass a little, both of them took audible deep breaths. They couldn't see the smile on my face, but it was damn sure stretching from ear to ear. I felt fingers fumbling with the clasps on my bra and suddenly, my titties were out. I turned back around to find Ashlei standing right up on me, breathing hard while licking her lips. There was very little space in between her and me, but there was enough room to touch, so that's what she did. With deliberate slowness, she used both of her hands to grab my titties and caress them firmly. The goosebumps arose on my flesh instantly as my body remembered our past moments of intimacy in vivid detail.

"Your skin is still the softest I've ever felt," Ashlei whispered, smiling seductively.

"I'll tell you the secret to it once we're done," I replied, pulling her towards me.

My mouth sought hers hungrily, not bothering to wait for permission before my tongue shot from in between my lips to greet her. The taste of raspberry on her tongue invaded my mouth, fueling my hunger on a different level and making me crave more of her sweetness. My hands began to wander under her t-shirt until I came into contact with the taut flesh of her flat stomach. Just rubbing on her had my pussy pounding like two bass drums, and the beat only increased as my hand moved lower into her jeans.

"Mrs. Snow, you have a guest."

All motion immediately ceased as Ashlei and Mo looked around curiously, trying to pinpoint where the voice was coming from. With reluctance, I walked over to the intercom just inside the bathroom door.

"Who is it?" I asked impatiently.

"A Ms. Toreno. She says she's your client, but you weren't expecting a house call this evening."

"That's for damn sure," Mo said, shaking her head in annoyance.

"Tell her I'll be out in five minutes," I said, already reaching for my clothes.

"Seriously, Snow?" Ashlei asked, with obvious disappointment.

"You know it's always business before pleasure when it comes to me. I need to speak with her about what happened earlier, and since she didn't answer any of my calls, now seems like the perfect time to get answers," I explained, dressing swiftly.

"Do you want me to go with you?" Mo asked.

"Nah, I want you to get the party started with this one, because she looks beyond sexually frustrated," I said chuckling.

"You ain't never lied," Ashlei said, pinching my nipple quickly.

"I can take care of that, but you just make sure you keep your ears open, so you can hear what that bitch is not saying," Mo said.

I nodded my head in understanding, and then gave both women a quick peck on the lips, before leaving them in the bathroom. I grabbed my all-black Berretta 9mm from my bedside table and tucked it into the back of my slacks as I walked out of the room and down the stairs.

"Where are you going, Mom?" Junior asked, appearing out of nowhere.

"I'm gonna run to the store really quick, but I'll be back before you have a chance to miss me. Do you want me to bring you anything?"

"No, just you," he replied, giving me a hug.

I couldn't help smiling at his reply, because it was just further proof my little man wasn't like most kids. He enjoyed his material possessions and toys, but he knew I outvalued all of that shit because I was his mother. For him to realize that made me feel like I was doing my job as a parent, and it wasn't easy, given the double-life I'd chosen to lead. It was worth it though.

"I got you, baby boy, now go back to your girlfriend."

"Moooommmm!" he whined, clearly embarrassed.

I laughed at the slightly mortified expression on his face as I headed out the door. I was still laughing as I slid behind the wheel of my truck and backed out of the garage. I loved my son more than anything in the world and it was because of that, that by the time I'd gotten to the front gate of my community, I had the look of a killer firmly in place. I'd almost lost my life today and before this night was over, I determined to find out how that happened.

"Get in," I demanded, pulling up alongside of Phillisa's green Porsche 911. I spotted the two all-black Hummers sitting off to the side, and I knew this was her security, but she got in without hesitation and I pulled off.

"I'ma start off by telling you the disappearing act you pulled today, damn near got a price put on your head," I stated honestly.

"I can understand that, and I'm so sorry you almost died. I say that with complete sincerity. The reason I came to see you personally is because I wanted to look you in the eyes and tell you the situation has been handled. The person who made that call did it without checking with me, but I promise you that was his last call. I'm sure you can understand mistakes happen sometimes."

"Mistakes? Yes. A nigga disobeying my orders or dropping the hammer on somebody without my permission? Absolutely not! I smell bullshit, Phillisa."

At first, my response elicited no reply from her, and we rode on in silence but I could tell she was thinking hard as fuck.

"You know, I can see why Zion loved you the way he did. Before you accuse me of switching subjects, or trying to deflect, let me explain. The more I get to talk to you, the more I get to see how your brain works, and it's honestly a beautiful thing."

"Flattery will get you nowhere in this game, sweetheart, except an early grave fucking with me," I said, smiling at her.

"That's my point, I almost did end up in that early grave. You see, you're one hundred percent right that niggas under my command don't harm the hair on a motherfucker's head without me giving the nod. This move against you was an absolute renegade move, an attempted coupe to move me out of power. I knew my father had to have some help when it came to setting me up, and I had a few suspicions about who it was. After the move was made on you, I confirmed who the traitor was, eliminated the others just in case they got any ideas, and now here I am with you, coming to plead my case. I'm not trying to go to war with you, Claudette."

"Aren't you though? How do you not see that by taking on Campa, you're gonna pull me into a war along with him? In case you didn't know, it was him that pulled my ass out of that, and you're smart enough to know that, Phillisa. My team follows my lead the way they do because my loyalty is unwavering, so how is it gonna look for me not to ride with Campa when the time comes? It sounds to me like you're trying to create a situation of complete mutiny and anarchy so you can destroy us both, while you pick up the pieces."

"There's that beautiful mind at work again, but this time you're giving me too much credit, sweetheart. I'm not here for you, and—"

"And that may be true, Phillisa, but if I'm collateral damage it's all the same. Dead is dead!"

"That's the point I'm trying to make to you, but you refuse to see the big picture!" she said, throwing her hands up in exasperation.

"Well, help me see the big picture then, with your smart ass."

"It's simple, for real. We kill Campa and take over everything that's his," she stated calmly.

My first response was to chuckle until I looked over at her and saw she was dead ass serious.

"So, you want me to believe your friends are just gonna welcome his successor, even though I don't break bread at your table?" I asked.

"That's exactly what you should believe, except I think you missed the part where I said we take over everything that's his."

Her words rolled around in my head until I was forced to pull over at the sandwich shot and put the car in park so I could turn and face her.

"What are you talking about?"

"You heard me, Mrs. Snow, and you know it's the right move to make. How long did you really think you could exist in his shadow before you either became a threat, or outgrew him? Furthermore, you know Campa, so either of those options results in you being put in a fifty-five-gallon oil drum and dropped in the deepest part of the ocean. You've seen that shit up close and personal, so there's no reason for you to be naïve or willfully ignorant. Think, Claudette!"

Her words made me do just that, because I knew she was telling me the truth I wished I could ignore. Campa may have saved my life, but it only made sense for him to do that, so I wouldn't be looking for him to be the one to turn around and split my potato. Wasn't it a rule of the street that the closest motherfucker to you was the one who could do the most damage? Tony had been the closest one to me, but he had also been an obstacle for Campa to move out of the way, because he never would've betrayed me. Just thinking about the fact that my brother from another mother was no longer here with me, hurt me enough to still bring tears to my eyes.

"So, I'm supposed to trust you…the woman who's about to kill her own father?" I asked seriously.

"That man ain't my father and he hasn't been since the day he murdered the love of my life."

"Ah, so that's what this is all about? He took the man you loved, and now you want revenge," I said, nodding my head in understanding.

It seemed that us voicing what happened brought her pain to the surface, because I could suddenly see it, almost like looking in the mirror. I knew how deep that well of pain went, and that it could destroy you if you let it be your guide.

"You gotta be careful about letting that particular monster motivate you, sweetheart," I said.

"Speaking from experience?" she asked.

I nodded my head in response to her question as I sat back in my seat and stared through the windshield at a night that existed long ago. If I closed my eyes, I could still taste the meal I'd prepared for Zion…and I could feel his lips on my pussy. For a brief moment, I thought I was tripping because I could feel his fingers walking along my collar bone right now. I opened my eyes, expecting to see him sitting next to me, but instead I was staring into the twin pools of desire that belonged to Phillisa.

"Wh-what are you doing?" I asked softly.

"Nothing."

She spoke softly, seductively, but her eyes remained intense and her hands stayed busy, working their way under my shirt. By the time she got to the flesh right in between my titties, it was hard for me to breathe.

"Phillisa, what-what are you doing?"

"Asked and answered, Counselor."

The fog that clouded my brain was one of confused arousal. My body had a mind of its own, and it was responding to her touch like we were old lovers. The throb of my pussy was strong and insistent, but my mind was still trying to grasp what was happening in this moment. It was a natural reflex for me to look around to see if we were being observed by anyone, and that's when I noticed the same two Hummers sitting about fifty feet away. Aside from that though, there was no other vehicle in the parking lot with us.

"Phillisa, we-we can't do this."

"Give me one good reason why," she replied, letting her hands roam lower until she was inside my slacks, rubbing my clit in slow circles.

"Be-be-bec-c-cause you're-oh, wow."

I was really trying to put together a coherent thought, but she was purposely making that impossible by pushing two fingers inside my tight pussy and swirling them in clockwise circles like she was stirring my confection to just the right finished product. In my mind, I had the best of intentions to stop this just because it was crazy, but the song she was playing inside me had me ready to sing! Before I could stop myself, I'd turned in my seat so that she could get a better angle for sliding her fingers in and out of me. While she worked with a steady rhythm with one hand, she used her other hand to unbutton my pants. My body flooded with disappointment when she pulled her fingers out of me, but it was quickly replaced by more desire when she pulled my pants down over my hips.

"I like that you don't wear panties, because that's how I always envisioned you," she whispered.

I kept my mouth shut so I wouldn't reveal the reason why I wasn't wearing panties, because it was irrelevant to here and now. When she had one leg in and one leg out of my pants, I cocked my leg up on the back of my seat, so she could get a good look at my pretty pussy.

"Mmm, may I?" she purred softly.

"Only if you know what you're doing."

Her soft laughter filled the car, but it was cut short when my lips met hers and the conversation got deeper. The first lick she took was long, slow, lazy, and it froze my breath in my chest. By the second lick, I was reaching for her head, but she swiftly pinned my hands together and held them so I couldn't touch her.

"Let me show you I know what I'm doing. I'ma make it snow."

The sound that came from my throat as she began sucking on my clit was foreign to my ears, and I had to remind myself to hold onto my pride. It only took ten minutes, and two orgasms that were comparable to nothing in my memory banks, for me to say fuck that pride!

"Ph-ph-phuck!" I moaned loudly.

I could feel her pinkie moving steadily in and out of my tight asshole, adding the third ring to the circus that was her fingers in my pussy. No one except Zion had made my pussy rain juices and cum, but the third time Phillisa made me climax, she shattered the myth. The feeling was so intense that I could feel the tears rolling down my cheeks, but I was helpless to do anything to stop them. I wanted her to stop touching me, as aftershock after aftershock held me under the waters of climactic siege, but she simply continued to drink from me like her favorite wine glass. It was a full fifteen minutes later when the shaking in my body subsided enough for me to pull my legs from around her neck, but I still wasn't in any position to move around.

"Jelly…I feel like fucking jelly," I said, chuckling softly.

She laughed with me while leaning back in her seat and staring openly at me.

"I've wanted to do that since the first time I saw you."

"And here I thought you were worried about maintaining your freedom the first time you saw me," I replied.

"That day in the courthouse wasn't the first time I saw you, Claudette. I've known who you were for years, I just never had a reason to approach you."

I stared at her for a moment and thought about what she was saying to me. Undoubtedly, she'd seen me before because Zion was proud of the bad bitch he had, but he also would've made it clear that anyone approaching me without his permission, would result in some bad shit happening.

"That makes sense, I guess. I won't lie though. I did appreciate your beauty that first day I saw you in the courthouse. Zion is the last man I was ever with, so it's women who turn me on and you're definitely a head turner. Had I known back then you could eat pussy like that though, you would've come home with me right then!" I said, laughing.

"Wait, you ain't had no dick since Zion died? Not even a friendly fuck with Tony occasionally?"

I don't know why her question irritated my soul so much, but immediately stopped laughing.

"Tony was my best friend, not my fuck buddy. Furthermore, this pussy will never see another dick besides Zion's," I said, maneuvering around to put my pants on.

"I wasn't trying to offend you, Claudette, I was just genuinely surprised. I know I shouldn't have been though, because you're nothing if not loyal, and I can tell that you really loved Zion."

"Love Zion. I love Zion, so don't get that confused in any way. I fuck with females just to scratch that itch, but my heart will always belong to Zion Snow, and Zion alone," I stated aggressively.

"Okay, sweetheart, okay."

She held her hands up in surrender, or maybe it was to signify a truce. Either way I didn't say anything else about that subject, I just pulled my pants on and fixed myself up. I didn't like the awkward silence that filled the car, but I didn't say shit to break it.

"I'm sorry, Snow, but I'm not sorry about what just happened here. I meant it when I told you I've wanted to taste you since the first time I saw you, and I hope that's not the only time you allow me that pleasure."

"You think I'ma let you turn me out with that tongue of yours, huh? Nah, boo, you got me fucked up!"

Her laughter was loud and genuine, which made me laugh in turn. We both knew she had some killer head, and I knew it wouldn't be hard to become a slave to that shit, if I wasn't careful. I wasn't going out like that.

"I ain't trying to turn you out, Snow…but I'm not gonna turn down the option of making you mine, because we would be unstoppable on all levels."

I let her statement hang in the air as my mind processed it from different angles. She'd spoken a lot of truth before our sexual encounter, which meant I needed to admit my days with Campa were numbered. It was always better to choose your next career move than to have it chosen for you.

"I heard all the truth you spoke, so…"

My statement was interrupted by her phone ringing. I had no idea who was on the other end, but the way her demeanor changed when she got a look at her phone's screen made me think it was her dude. She sent the first round to voicemail, but within thirty seconds, it was ringing insistently again.

"Hold on a second," she said, opening the passenger side door as if to step out.

"I'm not gonna say shit while you talk, you're good."

She hesitated for another moment, but finally the ringing phone won her attention and she closed the door again.

"What's up, baby?" she answered smiling.

"Hey, Mom, I just wanted to know when you're coming home."

"I'll be home soon, baby, I promise. You just keep being a good boy for me, okay?" she asked sweetly.

"Yes, ma'am."

"Okay, I'll call you back when I get back to my hotel room. I love you, little man."

"I love you too, big mama," he replied laughing.

I could tell this was an obvious running joke with them, and I hated to intrude on their moment. She hung up the phone and looked out the passenger side window for a few moments without saying anything.

"It's hard being here when you'd rather be there, trust me, I know," I said empathetically.

When she turned towards me and looked in my eyes, I could feel her sadness, but it was more than that though. It seemed like regret lived inside her too, and that was also something I could understand.

"Campa doesn't know about him, does he?" I asked.

"No, and—"

"You don't gotta worry about saying shit. Like you said before, I know Campa, so I know he's capable of the unspeakable shit that goes bump in the night. My lips are sealed," I said.

"That's not enough though, Claudette. I need your help to ensure the future for our kids. If not you, then who else will help me do it?"

I knew the answer to her question just as well as she did, but what she was asking wasn't as simple as picking a side. People were gonna die behind this shit, a lot of people were gonna die. That didn't bother me though, because if the choice was between me and mine, and somebody else's, then there was no choice.

"I hope you've got some type of plan, Phillisa, because this shit is gonna get ugly."

"Real ugly," she agreed.

Chapter 15

Two months later
Bogotá, Columbia

"Buenos dias, señora, what would you like to drink with your breakfast?"

"I'll have whatever she's having," I replied, nodding to-wards Phillisa's glass on the table.

"Right away, ma'am."

The waiter disappeared, leaving us at the table alone, staring at each other silently.

"How did you sleep?" she asked calmly.

"Fine…and you?"

"It would've been better if you were in bed with me, but I managed to get a few hours," she replied.

"Under normal circumstances, I probably would've joined you, but this is a business trip and I know I need to make the right impression on your people. Somehow, waking up with the taste of your pussy on my tongue, doesn't strike me as how they want us handling business."

She chuckled softly while taking a sip from whatever was in her glass, but she nodded her understanding of what I was saying. I'd come to Columbia to sit down with the connect to solidify our new relationship before I set fire to the old one, and I knew I needed to be completely focused on business. In the past couple months, I'd become somewhat addicted to Phillisa's head game, but I'd levelled the playing field by putting my smash game down too. So, it was kinda awkward to be sleeping under the same roof, but to be doing it in separate beds, because we'd gotten used to other things.

"Are you nervous?" she asked suddenly.

"No, not really. I mean, I know that they know who I am, and I wouldn't have made it this far if they weren't as interested in this arrangement as I am. I'm looking at this like it's all a formality for real."

"Good, because you're right. The real test has been these last two months, because they've been watching how you operate under pressure," she stated.

The waiter reappeared and sat my glass on the table, along with a plate of delicious smelling food.

"I took the liberty of ordering for you," Phillisa said, smiling.

I took a sip of the mimosa to hide my smile and gather my thoughts, so that I wasn't focusing on the romantic side of Phillisa's personality. For me, the biggest test over the last couple months had been to keep everything about us a secret. Campa still didn't know that I knew who she was to him, or anything about the problems that existed between them. As far as he knew, my relationship with Phillisa had ended on the day I got her case thrown out, and that's exactly what we wanted him to think. In all actuality though, she and I had been laying the groundwork for the biggest takeover in history. It hadn't been easy either. I'd had to take the product she was getting from her connect, and I'd had to create a new market for it somewhere where I wasn't pumping the work that I got from Campa. The quality was so similar, it was impossible to tell what was coming from where, so selling it wasn't an issue. Having to tap into new markets made me nervous, just because I didn't like operating on territory that was unfamiliar to me. With the help of my team though, we'd pushed coke, heroin, pills, and synthetic drugs from South America through North America, around to Central America and back. I was literally making so much money that I was scared, but I didn't let that fear consume me or stop me, because there was no looking back. Campa didn't operate like anything had changed between him and me, but I knew it had because I couldn't look at him and not see what he'd done to Tony. I didn't mention it to him though. I simply made money with him.

"So, what's on the agenda for today?" I asked, picking up my fork and digging into my food.

"We've got a meeting in about an hour, and then you'll head back home. I wanted to get this official sit-down out of the way so that you don't gotta worry about coming back out here unless you want to. It works better for everyone that we're self-sufficient, but there needed to be at least a sit-down so that there could never be a misunderstanding about any of this."

"So, what are you expecting them to say to us?" I asked.

"Nothing major, just that if we fuck up, we're gonna die horrible, painful deaths. You know, the usual."

She was smiling when she said this, but we both knew how serious this shit really was. I'd learned long ago that the connect was never forgiving when it came to the money or the product, and that's why I was the way I was.

"Are you going back with me?" I asked curiously.

"Are you asking because you want me to?"

"Don't answer a question with a question, Phillisa."

"Oh, so that's what we're doing? Okay. The simple answer to your question is no, not right now, but it's not because I don't want to. I need to spend some time with my son."

I nodded my head in understanding. There had been many days and nights in the past two months when I'd had to leave the business up to her, so I could spend time with Junior. For adults, time worked wonders for healing wounds, but for children it tended to hurt a little longer. I had no intention on rushing Junior to get over losing Tony, and I really didn't care what I had to sacrifice to be there for him. I was just lucky that I had a solid team around me to pick up the slack when necessary. Phillisa didn't have that, so she'd been missing out on a lot when it came to her son, and I felt for her when it came to that.

"Make sure you love on him extra hard for all the days and nights you've missed," I said smiling.

"Most definitely. I'll be back in the states before you have a chance to miss me though, so don't get any ideas of replacing me in your bed."

She smiled when saying this, but I could see the seriousness in her eyes.

"Trust me when I tell you, my focus is on business right now. I've gotta call a meeting and make sure my team is all on the same page."

"Do you think Campa knows anything?" she asked.

"No. I've made sure everybody is moving the same way we've always been moving. When it came to all the people I eliminated, I explained that away as them failing at their duties for one reason or another, so he doesn't suspect anything. I've done my best to appear nonthreatening to him, but I know he's gotten word there's a new player in the game."

"How do you know he knows that?" she asked curiously.

"He told me to be on the lookout for a drop in our out-of-town sales, because he wants to know if even one unit less is moving. The only time he makes that request is when we're not the only game in town, and he's trying to figure out if the new wave is gonna hurt his pockets. If it does, then it's elimination time."

"If he only knew," she said, smiling widely.

Despite the fact that I was smiling with her, I was ever conscious of the saying that those seeking revenge should dig two graves. I knew we had to be careful with the moves we were planning to make or run the risk of shit going to hell faster than any bullet. We ate the rest of our meal making idle chitchat, mixed with the occasional sexual commentary that got us all hot and bothered. When she got a text on her phone though, the mood changed and I knew the time had come. She paid the tab and led the way outside to the black Range Rover that had been waiting on us. From the time we'd stepped off the plane, I'd felt how much power came with Phillisa and her people. Everywhere we went, we were chauffeured and no matter where we went, we were never searched for weapons. I didn't ask how far up the food chain this shit went, but it was obvious that my decision to fuck with these people meant an upgrade.

"How good is your Spanish?" she asked, once we were in the backseat, moving swiftly to an unknown destination.

"I mean, it's passable, why?"

"Because these conversations will take place entirely in Spanish, and I need to know if you need me to translate," she replied.

"No, I should be good, but if I need your help, I'll look at you."

She nodded and focused her attention on her phone. Since I didn't know how long our journey was, I decided to do the same thing so that I was getting work done. It was about an hour and a half later, when the Range Rover came to a stop in front of a huge mansion in the middle of nowhere.

"You ready?" she asked, looking over at me intently.

"Yeah."

My response didn't require a moment of hesitation or thought, but she continued to stare at me like I was battling my nerves or something. I guess she was finally satisfied with what she saw, because she opened the door and led the way up the stairs. The front door was opened before a fist was ever raised to knock on it, and a beautiful young Latina led us inside. The interior of the mansion was tasteful, beautiful, and bold all at the same time, with the color scheme of deep burgundy, gold, and green. One thing I knew for sure was that I'd stepped into money that was different from riches. This was wealth. Phillisa and I followed our escort into a conference room, where eight sets of eyes sat staring back at us. I stood stone still, while she was greeted like a long-lost daughter by this room full of distinguished older men. I was amazed at the amount of love they displayed because it seemed out of place. I wasn't about to question or criticize it though. After they welcomed her home, they insisted that she sit, and then all eyes turned towards me. I felt slightly self-conscious, but I did my best not to let that show, because at the end of the day I was a boss bitch, and everybody sitting here knew that.

"So, you're the infamous Claudette Snow?" one man asked me.

"I am."

"You say that with incredible pride. Do you think that's wise?" another man asked.

I contemplated his question for a moment while also evaluating the fact that so far, only English had been spoken, despite Phillisa's warning.

"I do say that with pride and yes, I do think that's wise. My husband made his name ring before he died, and I've made sure to preserve the respect that's attached to it. We've earned that respect, and where it hasn't been given, I've taken it because it means just that much," I said calmly.

No one spoke immediately following my statement, but when I locked eyes with Phillisa, I could see the approval dancing in her beautiful orbs, so I knew I hadn't said anything wrong.

"Take a seat, Mrs. Snow, and let's get down to business," the first man instructed.

I breathed a slight sigh of relief as I took a seat, but I knew I'd just stepped off the diving board into the deep end. The question now would be could I swim with these sharks? For two straight hours, I was interviewed and interrogated, but by the time it was over, I knew the respect I'd spoken about was now established between us. At the end of our conversation, I was asked to leave the room, and I had a flashback to the movie *Scarface*. I didn't think I'd end up swinging from a helicopter by a rope, although one could never be too sure. While I waited out front by the Range Rover, I called Mo to let her know how I thought the meeting went. We chatted for a minute and made plans for her to pick me up from the airport when I touched back down. Phillisa reappeared just as my call ended, but I couldn't interpret anything from her facial expression.

"Let's go," she said, climbing into the back of the SUV ahead of me.

I followed her lead, and we got on our way. As badly as it was eating at me to know what was said after I left, I didn't say shit, nor did I look at her expectantly. Instead, I texted Junior and told him to set up Fortnite for us so we could play together from my phone. One thing I loved about technology these days was that I could interact with my son from anywhere in the world of gamers. I made sure to put my headphones in, so nobody would hear the other gamers talking shit, or my son talking it back.

"So, you're gonna act like you can't hear me now?" Phillisa asked a few minutes later.

"What did you say? I'm playing a game with Junior," I replied, never taking my eyes off my phone's screen.

"I said, you're in, bitch."

I suppressed the scream that wanted to erupt from my throat and remained nonchalant as I kept playing the game.

"That's what's up," I said.

"Really? That's all you have to say about the monumental shit that's about to take place?"

"I mean, what am I supposed to say, Phillisa? I knew they were gonna fuck with me, so it's not a surprise."

Her laughter was loud and bubbly, and it was contagious. We laughed until tears rolled down our cheeks, and then we hugged until the sexual tension between us ratcheted up a notch. When I pulled back and looked at her, I could tell we were thinking the same thing, but we were both smart enough to know not to trust the driver with this secret.

"We have to go out to dinner and celebrate," Phillisa said.

"I'm with that, but I wanna head back home tonight."

"I got you, we'll just spend the day together," she replied, smiling seductively.

I didn't say another word on that subject, I just went back to my game with Junior. My son and I laughed, joked, and shot people until the SUV pulled up in front of the hotel. After I promised to see him soon, he let me get off the phone, and we stepped out into the beautiful afternoon sunlight.

"So, what do you wanna do?" I asked, looking at Phillisa.

"This country is so beautiful and the next time you come here, I'm gonna give you the grand tour. Right now though, I'm gonna show you the inside of my hotel room, so I can see the inside of you."

"Lead the way, boo," I replied readily.

We made it upstairs and into her room within a few minutes and after that, I lost all track of time. I stopped counting after three orgasms a piece, but we definitely didn't stop what we were doing. The fight for dominance was serious, but in the end we both surrendered to each other repeatedly. It was close to midnight by the time I actually climbed aboard the private jet that would take me home, and as soon as I stretched out on the leather couch, I was dead to the world. I awoke to the pilot telling me to strap in for our landing. Once the plane touched down, I pulled my phone out to call Mo, and that's when I saw all the missed calls from her.

"Where the fuck are you, bitch?" she asked as soon as she answered.

"I just landed. Why, what's up?"

"I'll be there in twenty minutes."

Before I could ask her what the hell was going on, she'd hung up in my ear, and she declined all of my calls. I tried calling Ashlei, but I didn't get an answer from her either, and that's when I started to get worried. When I called Silk's phone it went straight to voicemail, and the worry I felt shot up to straight fear, because Silk always answered his phone. The only way he wouldn't answer is if it was physically impossible. I quickly made my way off the plane and through the airport, still trying to call Silk the whole time. By the time I got out front, Mo was sliding to a stop in her BMW, and I got in immediately.

"Why the fuck ain't Silk and Ashlei answering their phones?" I asked.

"I don't know about Ashlei, but Silk...Silk is in trouble."

"What kind of trouble, Mo-Mo?" I asked impatiently.

"The kind you don't get a bond for."

Aryanna

Chapter 16

"Bond? What the fuck happened that he would need a bond, Mo?"

"Apparently, he shot somebody a while ago, but they couldn't prove the person was dead or something. Now they can," she replied.

"Something don't sound right, Mo, so what am I missing?"

Her response was to put the car in gear and pull off fast into traffic. I didn't know what she was trying to work up the nerve to say, but her silence was about two seconds away from pissing me the fuck off.

"Look, Snow, I tapped into my sources to find out what I could, but I'm running into roadblocks and that's why I was blowing your damn phone up. Obviously, you were too busy to respond though."

I didn't have to look at her to know I was hearing some animosity in her tone, but I wanted to make sure that the reason for it was what I thought it was.

"So, you're mad because I was out handling business, or is it who I was handling business with?" I asked.

"I don't give a fuck about you handling business because that's what you're supposed to do."

The fact that she left the rest unsaid really said it all, but I didn't take the bait right away. Instead, I chose to ride on in silence for a while and try to figure out what to do about Silk, because he was my priority. I wouldn't know how bad it was until I spoke with him, but something about the timing of this shit didn't feel right at all.

"So, what's your problem with Phillisa?" I asked finally.

"You're trusting her with too much too soon, and I think you're blinded by whatever physical hold she has on you."

"I'm sorry, did you just say the pussy or head has me open to the point that I'm making life changing mistakes?" I asked, sure that I'd heard her wrong.

"Is that what you heard me say?"

"That's damn sure what it sounded like, Mo."

"Oh, okay."

The fact that she left it just like that, made me wanna back hand her ass in the face right then, but I resisted that urge and instead chose to try and understand what she was saying.

"You've got my attention, Morano, so go ahead and explain that bullshit you spoke."

"It's only bullshit because you don't wanna see it, Claudette. You just met this bitch, but you've already got her so deep in your business, she could put a bullet in your brain and take over before your body got cold. Does that seem like some shit you would ordinarily do? Absolutely fucking not! So, the only conclusion I can reach is that the head must be fire. Am I right?"

"Fuck you, bitch! Ain't nobody got me open, pussy whipped, head whipped, or any goddamn thing in between! I'm making business moves according to what needs to be done right now, and I've kept you in the loop every step of the way, so you know I'm speaking truth. However, if at any time you feel like you don't wanna follow my lead, then you're free to move the fuck around and explore your employment opportunities elsewhere," I said sincerely.

"I noticed you didn't deny the fact that you're fucking shorty though, so maybe you're not seeing what I'm saying, because you're too close to the situation. Just food for thought."

I opened my mouth to verbally hop on her ass again, but I couldn't deny the point she'd just made. I hadn't wanted to lie to Mo, because we didn't do that. I knew she fucked with other people because she wasn't full-time lesbian, but I didn't question her about it, nor did I judge what she did. All I asked for was the same in return.

"Who you fucking right now, Mo?"

"What?" she replied, bewildered.

"I asked who you're fucking, because I wanna see if that relationship is fucking with your judgement."

"Oh, so you think I'm just pulling shit out of thin air now, huh? Well, all you gotta do is holla at Ashlei, and then you can face the harsh thing called truth, with your ignorant ass," she said sarcastically.

I knew there was no point in arguing for real, so I decided to keep my mouth shut to avoid us having a falling out. Instead, I chose to focus my energy on finding out what I could about Silk and why he was locked the hell up on a cold case. I pulled my phone out and went to work on my contacts, both legal and illegal, trying to get some type of picture painted about the whole situation. By the time we'd pulled up in front of Mo's house, that bad feeling I had about there being some fuckery amiss had increased dramatically.

"Look, it's too late for me to go home and deal with this, so if you don't mind, I'm just gonna set up shop here at your house," I said.

"You know I don't care, Snow. I'll put on a pot of coffee and help you."

The darkness hid my smile, but I had no illusions that this gesture on her part pushed all the shit that was said up under the rug. We got out of the car and headed up the sidewalk to her front door. Before she could put the key in the door it was pulled open, but I didn't see anyone standing in the doorway. Mo didn't act surprised and she didn't break stride, so I followed her lead and walked through the door into the house.

"You wanted to know who I was fucking, well here he is. Fatz, this is Snow. Snow, this is Fatz."

"What's good?" he said, closing the door behind us, and locking it.

I took a moment to evaluate the nigga standing in front of me, almost laughing out loud because he was sooooo not her type. Morano dated pretty niggas, but this nigga in front of me would never be considered that by anyone's measurement. His name could've been midnight or navy blue if his skin complexion was any indicator, and he was covered in obvious prison tats, so I didn't have to wonder where they met. They only thing that stopped me from laughing outright was the look in his eyes. I knew enough killers, and there was no doubt in my mind that this nigga had multiple bodies under his belt. The dreadlocks made him look like a Haitian teddy bear, but there was nothing soft about dude, so I chose my words carefully.

"What are your intentions with Mo?" I asked.

Surprisingly, this question made him laugh, but the humor stopped just short of reaching his eyes.

"My intentions? Honestly, my only intention is enhancement because if I ain't adding to her life, then I'm in the damn way. I ain't like most niggas who come with nothing more than dick and disappointment though, because I believe in bringing something of substance to the table. So, you ain't got nothing to worry about, because your homegirl is in great hands with me."

"I hope you're telling the truth because if not, this shit only ends one way," I said.

"Now you're speaking my language," he replied, smiling in a sinister way.

"Stay focused, Snow, we've got work to do. Fatz, can you make us some coffee, baby?"

"You know I got you, love, just set up in the living room."

She gave him a thorough tonguing down before moving past him into the living room. I waited until I was sure we were out of earshot, and then I stood in front of her with my hands on my hips.

"What?" she asked with fake innocence.

"The fuck do you mean what, bitch? When did you start fucking with him, or maybe the better question is, when did he get out?"

"You're in my business now, Claudette, but I'll let it slide. I've been cool with Fatz for a while now, but he never jeopardized my position on the inside. We kicked it on some friendship-type time, and when he got out a few weeks ago, he hit me up to see what I was up to."

"Oh, so you're not fucking him?" I asked.

"No, I'm absolutely fucking him, but it's deeper than that with us, because he doesn't just wanna smash and pass. He wants me, and he appreciates who I am when I'm not on my back. That's more than I can say for most of the niggas I've fucked with in recent memory."

Given the fact that she and I were actually friends, I knew she was speaking truth, just like I knew how much it meant to her that there was a man who could actually see past her beauty to the woman underneath. Mo had a heart of gold, but being beautiful had forced her to be a bitch, so she wouldn't be taken advantage of or perceived as weak. I had real love for her, so I wanted her to have what Zion and I had had, which meant I couldn't prejudge her new nigga without knowing him.

"Does he make you happy?" I asked.

"Honestly, I don't know what happiness looks like, but I know he makes me look forward to tomorrow in a way nothing and no one has."

"Yeah…I know what that feels like," I replied wishfully.

"Are you hungry, Snow?" Fatz asked, coming into the room with two cups of coffee on a tray.

"Uh…no, I'm okay thanks," I replied.

He looked at me hard for a second before turning his attention to Mo and waiting.

"A couple sandwiches will be good, bae," Mo said.

"I got you, beautiful, and I'll bring you an edible too," he said, smiling at her.

I wanted to tell this fat, black nigga I'd been polite with my "no thank you" because he was about to rub me the wrong way, but I kept my mouth shut because of the look they were sharing. It didn't matter what I thought, because I could see the love between them two, and I wasn't even sure that they knew of its existence yet. All I knew was that Mo deserved it. When he walked from the room again, she turned to me, and I could see the justification on the tip of her tongue.

"Thanks bitch, because I am hungry after that long ass flight, but I didn't wanna impose on somebody I don't even know," I said.

"It's nothing, bae, he treats me like a queen, and would do anything to make me happy."

"I believe that for real…and I heard what you were saying to me in the car. I know I need to use more caution when it comes to introducing people into our circle, and I promise you I will," I vowed, raising my right hand like I was taking the stand.

"Oh, I know you will, because I'ma kick your ass if you don't. Now, let's get this shit with Silk figured out, because he is too fine to be locked up."

"Easy, bitch, I don't got time for no funny shit because it's clear in that nigga Fatz's eyes that he'll put somebody in the ground for you. I can't afford for him to be at my greatest asset in the street," I said.

"Oh bitch, you better know I ain't dumb enough to pit them two crazy motherfuckers against each other. I'm serious Claudette, I wouldn't do that, so you can stop looking at me like that. Are you-are you ok?"

I knew she was talking to me, because I could feel my mouth standing open, but my mind was suddenly racing a million miles a minute.

"I'm-I'm good, but I think I get it now," I said slowly.

"Get what, Snow? What do you get?"

"In the car, I told you something wasn't right about this shit with Silk, and that's the way I felt the whole time I was trying to track down leads on him. I know why it doesn't make sense now though…"

"Okay, Claudette, don't keep a bitch in suspense!"

"Silk and Jeezy are my two biggest advantages in the street, and anyone who's looking to start a war with me would know that, right? So they would be the first people that you gun for…only you won't gun for them if you're trying to move with stealth and surprise, you'd just remove them from the equation," I said, looking at her.

It only took a few seconds for the lightbulb to go off behind her eyes, and then I knew we were on the same page.

"When was the last time you heard from Jeezy?" I asked, already pulling up his contact info in my phone.

"I haven't talked to him since we were all together last, but I'm sure if something had happened to him that we would've heard about it."

I could see the doubt in her eyes as she made the statement, and it did nothing to relieve the sudden anxiety I was feeling. I quickly punched in his number and waited while it rang on the other end. After the first fifteen rings, I hung up and tried all over again, this time letting it ring a total of thirty-two times before accepting defeat. About the time Fatz was bringing in our sandwiches, I was checking everywhere between here and New York, looking for any sign of Jeezy. It wasn't until I actually reached out to our mutual friends in New York City that I got a second piece of news that further fucked up my night.

"I don't know what exactly is going on up top, but shit is in complete disarray right now, and nobody wants to talk on the phone. All I know about Jeezy is that he's been summoned home by the big homies, and he has orders not to speak to anyone that ain't blood," I said, sighing in frustration.

"So, what does this mean?" Mo asked.

"It means that if a war breaks out right now, we're the most vulnerable we've ever been."

"Ohhhh, shit!" she said, looking up at me like deer caught in the headlights.

"You'll be alright," Fatz said confidently.

"How the fuck do you know? You don't know shit about what the fuck is going on right now, nigga, so just keep your comments to your goddamn self," I stated angrily.

The way Mo's breath audibly got trapped in her throat, I knew she felt like I'd crossed the invisible line, but at this point I didn't give two fucks.

"I know you'll be alright, because you've got a new hitta on your team, and I ain't nothing like the rest. I'm gonna overlook how you just talked to me because for real, I know you're going through a lot, and you honestly don't know no better. So, let's stay focused on what's important, and that's the survival of you and everything you love. If someone has gone through the trouble of getting rid of your armies, then it's a safe bet a war is coming, and it's coming quick. Without your men, how prepared are you?" he asked.

"I don't understand the question," I replied, trying valiantly to check my anger and annoyance.

"I mean, do you have a war chest, and how easily accessible is it?" he asked.

I looked at Mo before I even thought about answering this question, because the trust required to answer this question had to be given by her. If I opened Pandora's Box and this nigga betrayed us in the end, I would have no choice except to kill Mo, and that's what my look conveyed. She nodded her head in understanding though, and so I turned my attention back to Fatz.

"I got plenty of money and favors, so right now all I'm lacking is able bodies to pull the trigger," I stated honestly.

"Say less, let me make some calls."

He gave Mo a quick kiss before leaving the room with his phone in hand.

"Mo, you better be sure about this," I said, staring at her.

"That goes the same way for your decisions involving ole girl too. Matter fact, now might be a good time to get her on the horn and update her on our situation."

"Not yet. If she is untrustworthy, then I don't want her knowing whatever we're planning in the way of how to survive the first wave of attack. We can handle this, just like we handled everything that came before her," I said.

"I feel that, but you gotta remember that before, we've always known what enemy we were fighting. That's not the case right now."

Her statement held a validity that I wished it didn't, because there was nothing more dangerous than fighting in the blind. At the same time though, I had a feeling we weren't as blind as our opponent might think.

"If I was gambling, I'd say it's Campa coming after us," I said.

I watched in silence as Mo contemplated that for a moment without speaking.

"I don't know, Snow. I mean, you've been moving real regular, so there's no reason for him to be suspicious of you at all."

"Who said he has to be moving against me because of something I've done? Why can't it just be time to take me out, because he thinks I'm completely sleeping on his snake-like qualities?" I asked.

The silence between us was full of careful thought and consideration, until Fatz came back in the room with the perfect quick solution.

"What kind of weed is that you're smoking?" I asked.

"It's called cookie milk, and that shit is fire!" he replied, inhaling sharply.

"Well, pass it, my nigga," I said, holding my hand out.

I thought he would've looked at Mo first again for directions, but instead he handed it to me, and so began the cipher. The three of us smoked until the amount of smoke in the room reminded me of a car being on fire. I sat alone on the couch with my thoughts once the two of them got up and disappeared into her back bedroom. I tried to focus on the problems in front of me, but the sounds coming from her room were hella distracting, and they started to become annoying. It wasn't until I realized I had my hand inside my jeans rubbing my clit, that I realized why I was so annoyed about them fucking. I was horny as shit! For a brief moment, I sat there unsure of what to do, but the weed made me bolder by the second, until I finally stood up and headed in the direction of the bedroom. At first, it was a little harder to make out the sounds of passion over the Trey Songz bellowing from the speakers, but as I got closer, Mo's voice crystalized. As soon as I raised my hand to knock on the door, her voice turned into a shrill screech I recognized as her reaching the point of no return. The envy that swelled up in my chest pushed proper etiquette out the window, and I just opened the door unannounced. I immediately locked eyes with Mo first and then Fatz, but neither of them paused in what they were doing. Mo was on all fours on the bed facing me, and he was behind her with a hand full of her hair, pulling it mercilessly while he plowed into her with incredible force. The way her titties jiggled and swayed had me hypnotized, but the way he was putting his pound game down had me mesmerized.

"Close the door or come in," he said.

I took a deep breath and considered the possibilities. Then I closed the door.

Aryanna

Chapter 17

"S-S-Snow!"

The sound of my name struggling to escape from in between Mo's lips made the hair on the back of my neck stand up straight. I wanted to cross the room to her bed, but my feet were rooted to the spot they were in, just inside her door. It was something about watching them in motion that was hypnotizing and beautiful, but so completely erotic that my pussy was jumping wildly.

"Snow-SSSSSnow," she sang out.

I could tell by the way her eyes rolled that she was cumming fiercely, and the way Fatz was stepping into each stroke told me he knew what was happening too. My eyes went to his, and I could feel his touch from across the room. Never had I been in a situation that made me miss dick…until this very moment. When I crossed the room to stand in front of Mo, I was telling myself I would only watch and nothing more. It seemed like the closer I got, the harder he fucked her, until she went from being on all fours to face down with her pretty ass in the air.

"Damn, Mo," I whispered, biting my lip in jealousy.

"It's-it's g-g-good," she moaned, unashamed by her obvious submission.

When he suddenly stopped, I realized I'd been holding my breath every time he dove deep inside her, almost like I was taking the dick. He didn't pull out of her, but he didn't move either, and I was confused for a second.

"Take your clothes off, Snow," he demanded huskily.

"Huh?" I asked, unable to hide my surprise.

"You heard me. Take-your-clothes-off!"

The tone of his demand had my whole body tingling, but I was still hesitant to do what he wanted. It wasn't until Mo opened her eyes and smiled at me that I actually got up the nerve to do what he wanted me to. Once I was completely na- ked, I stood there, waiting on my next instruction.

"Bring me a taste of you," he said.

"A-a taste of me. How am I supposed to do that?" I asked, slightly confused.

His response was to flash me a smile that could only be described as mischievous. I felt like it was a challenge though, and I wasn't one to back down from shit. I reached down in between my legs, parted my pussy lips, and dipped a finger inside my wetness. I made sure to really soak my finger before I stepped around to the side of the bed and held it out to him. For a moment he stared at me, and then without looking at my finger, he opened his mouth for me to put my finger inside. I could feel myself blushing, but I did it anyway. The way he sucked on my finger brought me to the threshold of climax instantly, and I wanted more.

"B-bae, fuck me!" Mo demanded impatiently.

"Shut up," he replied, smacking her on the ass hard enough to make her juicy booty wobble from side to side.

"Ooooo," she moaned loudly.

When he pulled backwards until only the tip of his dick was still inside her, I couldn't help looking down, and I wasn't disappointed. He may have been an ugly nigga, but his dick was beautiful. I watched in slack-jawed fascination as he pushed inside her slowly, only to slide back out quickly, much to her disappointment. When he pulled his dick all the way out of her I thought I might dive face first on it, but I didn't get the chance. I watched in amazement as he spit on her asshole, and then worked his way inside her gently until the two be- came one again. The first stroke was one of patience and love, but the second one made her grunt like her head would pop off. I'd never seen Mo get fucked before by anyone except a female, and that hadn't made me jealous, but seeing all of this had me hot.

"I-I want some d—"

I never got the rest of the sentence out of my mouth, because a loud explosion shook the ground and knocked me onto the bed. In an instant every sexual thought flew out of my mind, and I was scrambling for my clothes.

"Grenade!" Fatz yelled.

"Get the guns!" Mo said, scrambling off the bed and grabbing her clothes.

I got dressed with lightning speed while focusing on listening to whether or not the house had actually been breached. I could hear niggas at the front door, but it sounded like the reinforced steel was holding up for the moment.

"Here," Fatz said, appearing at my side with a Mossberg shotgun outstretched for me to take. I grabbed it, racked the slide, and prepared mentally for survival.

"Their trying to surround the house," Mo said, looking at her phone while pulling on her Nike boots.

"Blast through the back door as soon as you see somebody," Fatz said to me.

I nodded my understanding and left out of the room to man my position. It was literally seconds later when I saw a figure approach the door, and I let the shotty rock them out their shoes quick. Whoever it was didn't get up, but the bad side to this was there was now a big ass hole in the door.

"We gotta move out!" I yelled.

I never took my eyes away from the door while I waited for Mo and Fatz to bend the corner. A few seconds later, they came running down the hall towards me, and I opened what was left of the back door.

"I got your back," I said, letting Fatz move past me into the crisp night air.

159

Mo pulled up the rear. It was deathly quiet outside, but it seemed like as soon as Fatz went around the corner of the house the night came alive with gunfire. The sound of several submachine guns, as well as some high-power pistols rang out clearly across the night air, making my pussy twitch with a different excitement. Fatz wasted no time letting the twin Ruger .44 pistols clutched in his grip, go for all they were worth, and I didn't hesitate to step into the fight with him. I couldn't see everyone I was shooting at because it was pitch black outside, but the glow from their barrels made them easy targets.

"Get behind the wheel, Mo," I said, following Fatz's lead towards her car.

I made sure to take the MAC-90 she handed me when the shotgun ran out of shells, and I let those bullets fly as fast as I possibly could. I felt a few bullets whiz by my hand, but all that did was turn me on even more, while motivating me to withstand the kickback from the MAC with a smile on my face. We all made it to the car and jumped inside while bullets rained like hail all around us.

"I bet your ass is glad now that you listened to me and got this bitch armored," I said, laughing as she smoked the tires and sped away.

"You better bet on it, bitch!"

We all laughed hysterically while making our getaway, but we made sure to keep a lookout for more enemies.

"Well, I think it's official now, war has been declared," Mo said somberly.

I didn't respond verbally, but instead pulled out my phone and made the most important call of my life.

"This is Claudette Snow. Activate emergency protocol Leo. I repeat, activate protocol Leo!"

I listened to the correct response come back over the line, and then I hung up the phone with a sigh of relief.

"What the hell is protocol Leo, Claudette?" Mo asked.

We'd known each other for a long ass time, so I know it threw her to have to ask me something that she actually didn't know. There were no secrets between Morano and me, because I loved and trusted her implicitly, but some things had to stay between me and God.

"If I tell you, then I'll have to kill you," I replied.

"Very funny, bitch. You ain't been keeping shit from me, so I don't know what makes you think that now is a good time to start," she said seriously.

"It's nothing really, it's just a plan that I put into place for Junior."

I knew that my effort at sounding nonchalant fell short by the look that she was giving me in the rearview mirror, but I kept my mouth shut.

"Uh, don't you think that I should know what's going on with my godson, bitch?" she asked.

"Don't sound so insulted, Mo, because you know I trust you more than anyone on planet Earth," I replied.

"No offense taken," Fatz said sarcastically.

"With all due respect, my nigga, I just met you tonight. And yeah, you were about to be the only nigga since my husband to stick dick in me, but unfortunately, not even that will make me trust you. Trust is earned and forged through the fire," I said.

"Well, not to put too fine of a point on it, but we literally just came through the fire," he replied.

I actually had no argument for that response, so I chose to focus on Mo instead.

"Look, Mo-Mo, it would've been irresponsible of me not to have a plan in place for Junior, in case something happens to me, especially with Tony being gone. Despite the money I've put away, I have no illusions about how cruel the world will be to my son, so I had to do everything possible to make sure he was safe, no matter what. I know you can understand that."

"Of course I can, bitch…I guess I'm just a little hurt that I'm not part of whatever this plan is for him. I mean, he's my godson, and you're my…"

"I know I'm yours, Mo-Mo, and for that reason, I know that nine times out of ten when it's my time to go, your squirrely ass will be right beside me, riding shotgun through hell," I said, smiling.

"I guess that means we're all going then, because I'm not letting her go without me," Fatz chimed in from the backseat.

I could see all of Mo's teeth in the moonlight because she was smiling that hard, and that made me take her hand in mine.

"Fatz, I know we don't know each other, but I've got a good vibe about you. I definitely like how you handled business back there too, and that's gonna come in handy in the very near future," I said.

"Are we talking about the shooting or the fucking?" he asked, chuckling.

We all laughed at his smartass question, but I quickly brought it back to a serious note.

"The dick is gonna have to wait, my nigga, because right now shit is serious. What you said about neutralizing my army seems to be true, so I need to know if you've got niggas you can call to make the world shake?"

"Yeah, I know a few dudes that'll come through, all you gotta do is tell me when and where you want them to be."

After Zion had been murdered and I'd been forced to step into his shoes, I'd gone somewhat overboard on the protection for myself and my team. I had a number of safe locations to lay low at, and they were fully stocked with weapons, but until I knew whether or not it was Campa who made a move on me, I had to go off the grid.

"We gotta lay low at a spot that Campa doesn't know about," I said.

"I agree with you, bae, so let's—"

"Nah, that ain't the right move," Fatz said calmly.

He spoke with such confidence that I had to turn around in my seat and look at him.

"Would you care to explain that statement?" I asked.

"It's like this, if you think it's your people coming at you, then he doesn't know that you know about him. Shit, he might not even know that the hittas he sent missed their target, because they started with Mo's house first. It's looking like his plan was to get rid of everyone around you, so you would be completely vulnerable and on your own. So right now, we've got the element of surprise on our side, and we need to use it."

"It sounds like you're saying we need to run down on the plug, and if that's what you're saying, I can think of an easier way to commit suicide, my nigga," I said, looking at him like he had two heads on his shoulders.

"It ain't suicide because it's not a move he would expect for you to make. I'm sure that he knows you're a certified hitta in your own right, but he don't know that you know he wants you out of the way. Watch what I tell you, he's gonna call to check your temperature, as soon as the word gets back to him that his shooters missed everything. How you handle that call will dictate his next move against you," Fatz said.

I thought about what he was saying to me and applied it to the street knowledge I'd amassed over the years. Campa was absolutely a worthy opponent, so if I really did have the upper hand in this moment, then it was smart of me to take it back.

"Okay, so let's say you're right. We're gonna need more than just us to run up in a heavily guarded mansion," I stated.

"I'll make my calls as soon as you decide on our immediate destination," he replied.

I thought about it and said the first thing that came to mind.

"Why don't we go to your house?"

As soon as I said it, I wished I could have taken those words back, but that was impossible. The way Mo looked at me told me she thought my suggestion was just as crazy, but there was no way to undo what was said.

"My house? I'm cool with that," Fatz replied nonchalantly.

"Y-you're cool with that? Uh, exactly what house will we be going to, because we just left our house," Mo said, looking at him in the rearview mirror.

"Sweetheart, I never said I didn't have a place of my own, I simply expressed my desire to spend my every waking moment with you, rather than live somewhere else. I've got a house though."

"Where do you live?" I asked.

His response was to lean forward from the backseat so that he could tap in the information into the car's GPS system. When that was done, he sat back. I read the address, and then read it again, before looking over at Mo. The expression on her face was the same as mine but given the fact she was driving and paying attention to the road, I was the one who turned around to look at him.

"This may be a stupid question, but uh…are you sure that's your address?" I asked.

His laughter was instantaneous and genuine.

"I'm not gonna take offense to that question because I know it may be hard to believe, given the fact I just came out of prison. I went in with a little money though, and my baby mama flipped it until it was clean enough to buy some shit that appreciates in value," he replied.

"We weren't trying to insult you, it's just that your address is in my neighborhood and the world can't be that fucking small," I said.

"But it is, because that's definitely my house, and I know my daughter's mom and husband have lived there for a while now."

"What's your daughter's name?" I asked.

"Alexia, why?" he replied.

Mo looked at me and I nodded my head to let her know he was telling the truth.

"My son plays with your daughter daily…he's actually in puppy love with her," I said.

"I see," he replied.

The way he said those two words let me know that he was just like any overprotective father.

"Don't take this the wrong way, but does your daughter know you as her father, because—"

"Because she loves her stepdad and calls him dad? Yeah, she knows me as her dad, but he's been there for her when I was unable to be, so I will never step in the way of their relationship. He's a good man, and he's been good to my daughter, so I can't do anything except respect him for that. My baby mama and I have a platonic relationship that will never again be romantic, but for the purposes of this situation, I'm sure she won't have a problem with us showing up on her doorstep."

Mo and I exchanged another look that resulted in me hunching my shoulders, so she would know it was her decision.

"Do you think Campa will come for you at your house, Snow?" Mo asked.

"No, but I ain't willing to bet our lives on it either," I replied honestly.

"Fatz, how exactly is this gonna work out with your baby mama, her husband, and your daughter under the same roof, where you wanna take your new boo and her home girl?" Mo asked.

"Just trust me, it'll be okay. Besides, we'll only be there long enough to kill you, and then we can move on."

Chapter 18

"Yo, this shit is crazy," I said, sitting down on the couch in the basement of Vivianna's house.

"How do you think I feel?" Mo whispered out of the side of her mouth, sitting down next to me.

"I really appreciate this, Viv, and I promise we'll be gone by the time the sun comes up," Fatz said to his baby mama.

"You better be, Andrew, because if you're not, then you're gonna answer all the questions your daughter is sure to have if she wakes up and finds you here. Especially since you're here with them."

Part of me wanted to take offense at the way she said the word *them*, but since I'd known her on a casual level for years, I knew she wasn't on no bullshit. I had to put a hand on Mo's thigh to keep her from getting up though, because she didn't know Vivianna, and right now she was biased, because this was the woman her nigga had a baby with. There was something about the baby mama that could make even the most secure woman insecure. I didn't know if it was the thought that they could somehow one day reclaim the man we had as their own, or if it was as simple as knowing your nigga had put dick to this female and there was proof. Either way, the baby mama was a sore spot for any woman, and right now I felt for my girl. It didn't help that Vivanna was absolutely gorgeous either. I wouldn't dare tell Mo, but on a few lonely nights I'd gotten a nut while thinking about my thick, sexy ass neighbor.

"Alright, ladies, now that we've gotten the immediate problem resolved, it's time to get to the next part," Fatz said, coming over to us.

I was momentarily blinded by Vivanna walking her juicy ass back up the stairs, but once she was out of sight, I refocused.

"Uh, I'm gonna need you to clarify what you meant in the car about killing me," Mo said immediately.

"So, I was thinking about what I'd said about how things went next, based upon how Snow reacted to the news that someone had made a move against you. I had an idea. If whoever this Campa person is thinks you're dead, then we have an even bigger element of surprise."

"Okay, but how do we make him think Mo is dead?" I asked.

"That depends, do you have a connection in the police department out here?" he asked.

"Yeah," I replied.

"Alright, so what we need is someone to put in a call that says there was a woman shot and brought into the hospital, where she was pronounced dead. We feed misinformation we know will get back to your dude Campa, and then we wait for him to call you and check on you."

I could tell by the way that Mo was nodding her head that she was following the direction Fatz was thinking in, and she liked it. That made two of us.

"I know he'll call ASAP, if for no other reason than to offer me some hollow platitudes and condolences, before telling me what's next for our business," I said.

"Right, but before we do that, I need to get an arrival time for the friends I'm about to call, because I guarantee Campa wants to meet with you, and you're not walking into that blind," Fatz said, already pulling his phone out and standing up.

While he moved to the far end of the basement to handle his business, Mo and I huddled together to talk.

"I'll say this about Fatz, that nigga ain't got no hesitation in him when it comes to getting with the shit for you," I said.

"Yeah, I know. That nigga was like that on the inside too, girl. If a nigga dared to disrespect me, I wouldn't even get a chance to reply to the shit or check the motherfucker, because Fatz was on it. He wouldn't come to me and tell me that he was gonna handle it either, he would just do it, because gangsta's move in silence."

"That shit turned you on, didn't it?" I asked, snickering.

"You know it did, and then the dick turned me out, bitch!"

We both laughed as quietly as we could while giving each other high fives. He turned around and looked at us, but he didn't say shit, he just shook his head and got back to his phone call. Once I got my laughter under control, I pulled my own phone out, and made the necessary calls to make the world believe that Anastasia Morano was no longer a part of this cruel world. I didn't know who Mo pulled out her phone to call, but she hung up when she saw Fatz and I were done with our calls.

"Is everything in place?" she asked.

"My dudes are on the way. What about things on your end?" he asked, looking at me.

"Yeah, we're good. As far as everyone knows, Morano died about fifteen minutes ago from multiple gunshot wounds, and there are no suspects because so far, no one knows where the shooting took place," I replied.

"Good shit, now we need to get our arsenal together while we wait on you to receive your call from the boss," Fatz said.

"I've got a storage locker full of everything we could need or want when it comes to this war shit. We can take my truck and get it, but Mo has to stay here," I replied.

"Stay here? Why the fuck do I gotta stay here?" she asked with obvious displeasure.

I knew she was once again thinking about the female upstairs in bed who'd had the dick that she was now hooded on, but she wasn't thinking about the whole picture.

"Mo…you're dead, boo, so you can't just be riding around like Campa doesn't have eyes all over the city," I explained patiently.

The look on her face told me she wasn't trying to hear none of that shit, but I knew she understood the seriousness of the situation we were in now.

"It'll be okay, baby. I promise, we won't be gone long," Fatz said, pulling her into his arms, and kissing her forehead gently.

The way he looked at her made my heart flutter, because there was so much love being expressed without words, and it was beautiful. She stayed stiff in his arms for as long as she could, and then her soft ass melted like a snow cone on a hot summer day.

"You know how I feel about you, Fatz, and what we have is amazing. It's just that—"

"Bae, you ain't gotta say shit or explain yourself to me. I know how you feel and trust me when I tell you, you have absolutely nothing to be worried about when it comes to Vivianna, or any other woman. You're all I want and need in this life, and whatever comes next. Facts!"

"Just remember all this sweet shit you kickin at me when I get on your motherfucking nerves, nigga, because you know I can be a straight bitch," she replied, smiling in a serious way.

"Your bitchy side is what attracted me to you from the jump. It was that and the way you shut down the lame niggas who kept coming at you when I was on the inside."

"I would never disrespect you by giving another nigga my time, especially when it was so much better spent on you," she said genuinely.

"Aw, you two are so cute, it's fucking sick! Now can we please get back to killing those that need killing?" I interjected.

Fatz looked at me and smiled, but then he took his time kissing Mo so thoroughly, my mind flashed back to what I'd almost experienced in their bedroom. Once he finally released her from his clutches, she actually swooned, but steadied herself before she fell face-first on the floor.

"This floor may be carpeted, but that shit will still bite back if you hit it," I said, laughing.

"Fuck you, bitch!" she replied, sticking up her middle finger and laughing with me.

I was still laughing as I followed Fatz up the stairs and out into the slightly chilly night air.

"Which house is yours?" he asked, looking around.

I pointed to my estate, and he side-stepped so I could lead the way. I kept my eyes peeled the entire way to my back door, looking for anything while relying on my instincts to start screaming at me if something was out of place. After quickly punching in the new security code to deactivate my alarm, I put my key in, turned it, and stepped into the brightly lit kitchen.

"Damn, what the hell happened? Did you kill your cleaning lady?" he asked, looking around the kitchen.

"Nah, I activated the emergency code that meant drop everything, grab the essentials for survival, and get the fuck out of Dodge with my son. I kept money stashed in the kitchen cabinets and in the pantry just for that purpose, so when I made the call, my team did what they were supposed to do. That includes changing the code to my house alarm, because if the wrong one was entered, this whole motherfucker would've exploded inside of sixty seconds."

I expected some type of comment or commentary once I finished explaining myself, but instead he simply stood there staring at me with a look of unabashed respect and admiration.

"Well played," he said.

"Thank you. Follow me so we can get everything we need and get ready for whatever is coming next."

I went through my house, gathering up all the bulletproof vests I had, along with the few guns I kept hidden here, because those were legally in my name. After that was done, I made sure the cameras were working properly so the inside and outside were being monitored. I led the way into my garage, we hopped in my truck and rolled out. The storage unit I had, existed when Zion was still alive, but absolutely nobody knew about it except for me and Tony. It was only a half an hour away from my house, but because I drove around to make sure nobody was following me, it took us just under an hour to pull up at the storage rental company.

"How long is it gonna take your people to get out here?" I asked.

"The arrival times vary because they're coming from different spots. I'm expecting my niggas that are coming from Virginia to be here by mid-morning though."

"Where is the meeting spot?" I asked.

"I didn't set one yet, I figured you would have an option or idea about where the best spot is."

I gave what he was saying some more thought and said, "I'll get back to you. For now, let's grab this shit and get back to the house before Mo kills your baby mama in her sleep," I said, half-jokingly.

He chuckled along with me, but I could tell by the look in his eyes he knew he'd left a lit stick of dynamite back at that house. Right or wrong, I would always side with my girl Mo, but I hoped she could stay focused on the bigger picture right now. I unlocked the storage unit, and I could tell by the deep breath I heard from behind me that Fatz was impressed by my little toy collection.

"My husband always believed in staying ready so you didn't have to get ready."

"If you don't mind me asking, how long has it been since you lost him?" he asked softly.

My mind immediately went back to the last night I'd spent with Zion, and then the rude way the police had come to notify me a few short hours later. I still wished with all my might to be able to turn back the hands of time, but I knew that was as impossible as avoiding this war.

"It seems like yesterday…and I don't wanna talk about it," I replied curtly.

"Understood. Let's load up what we can, and if me and my homies need anything extra, we'll come back through."

I nodded my head in agreement, and quickly got to work picking out what I thought was appropriate. It took us about an hour to pick out what we wanted and load it up, but the essence of time really wasn't weighing on me, because my thoughts were with my beloved. The way my heart still beat faster at the mere thought of Zion, was as clear an indication as the stars in the sky that I was still completely in love with him. I never wanted to fall out of love either, but I did wish it wouldn't hurt so much. By the time we got back to Vivianna's house, Mo had fallen asleep on the couch in the basement, clutching her pistol. I made sure the safety was on before I nudged her awake.

"We got enough guns and shit to—"

My phone vibrating in my pocket interrupted my statement. I didn't have to look at it to know who was calling me, so I just answered.

"Yeah?"

"What happened to you calling me when you made it home safely?" Phillisa asked.

I could hear the annoyance in her voice, but I was more surprised to be hearing her voice at all, because I'd thought it was Campa calling me.

"Um, I'm sorry, boo, shit just kinda got crazy here," I replied, mouthing Phillisa's name to Mo so she would know who I was talking to.

"Crazy how?" she asked.

I noticed the quick change in her tone, and now it was worry I felt vibrating over the phone's line.

"Nothing that I can't handle, trust me. How are things with you and your little man?" I asked.

"He's great, just as beautiful and fun loving as ever, but don't try to change the damn subject, Claudette. What happened, and don't lie to me, because you know I've got eyes all around you."

"Don't threaten me, Phillisa, because I don't give a fuck who you've got around me. You must've forgot who the fuck you're talking to, so let me remind you real quick—"

"I didn't forget anything, Mrs. Snow, and I definitely wasn't threatening you with anything other than finding out the truth about what's going on down there. I shouldn't have to do that though, because you and I should be past that. Way past that."

"We are past that, it's just that...I don't like to be questioned like I'm a child. I know that you're concerned, and I appreciate that because I know that it comes from a genuine place."

She didn't immediately respond to my statement, but I could hear her breathing over the phone line, so I was sure she was still there. The look Mo was giving me wasn't helping matters, because I could see her frustration in every line on her beautiful face. I understood her feeling like I needed to be careful with Phillisa, but I knew I had to take that advice with a grain of salt, due to her jealousy.

"Listen, Claudette, I know that you're a boss bitch, El Jefa in your own right, but you've got people around you that care about you and would lay down their lives for you. You just became part of a family, mi familia, and we always protect ours, sweetheart. So, what's going on?"

Her persistence let me know avoiding her question was only gonna result in her doing something that was unnecessary on my behalf, so I bit the bullet.

"Morano is dead," I blurted.

"Dead how?" she asked slowly.

"From unnatural causes," I replied sarcastically.

A very loud silence hummed over the line for what felt like an eternity, making me wonder if she'd hung up or if she just didn't care.

"Don't do anything, Snow. I'm on my way."

Aryanna

Chapter 19

"What did she say?" Mo asked.

I looked up from the now disconnected phone in my hand to Mo, and then back down at the phone.

"I know that bitch didn't hang up on me," I said in disbelief.

"That's what it looks like," Fatz said.

"What did she say before she hung up?" Mo asked.

I ignored her question again and called Phillisa back. I wasn't surprised when I didn't get an answer, but I was getting more pissed off with every unanswered ring.

"Ugh! Bitches get on my nerves!" I growled through clenched teeth.

"I'ma try not to take offense to that…actually I am taking offense to that, because I told your ass about fucking with that bitch," Mo said, shaking her head.

The look I levelled at her told her to shut the fuck up quickly, and she caught it loud and clear. I turned my attention back to the phone in my hand and once again tried to call Phillisa back. Of course, she didn't answer, which further pissed me off to the point that I contemplated smashing my phone.

"Fuck it," I said, giving up in frustration.

I looked up to find both Fatz and Mo looked at me expectantly.

"I told Phillisa you were dead, and she said she was on her way here. I was trying to explain that I don't need her help, but I never got that far."

"She's in love already and she wants to be here for you. It's understandable," Mo said smiling.

"Fuck you, bitch!" I replied without smiling.

"Women, huh?" Fatz said.

This made both of us look at him, and suddenly nobody was laughing.

"Bad joke, my bad," he said, holding his hands up in surrender.

The sound of his Rick Ross ringtone going off shifted everyone's attention. He answered and stepped away to speak, leaving Mo and me standing there looking at each other.

"I'm not in love with her, Morano."

Mo didn't reply, but the look she was giving me told me she heard the same defensiveness in my voice that I did.

"Look, she's only coming back because I'm now considered part of her family," I said.

"All it took was that one meeting for you to be embraced like family…and you think that has nothing to do with the fact that you two are bumping pussy's?"

"I know it don't got shit to do with that because I've been by your side. All I'm saying is that I think you're being naïve if you really think there's no perk to fucking your new plug. And if there's a perk, then there's also a consequence if shit goes bad."

I let her words hang between us because they were nothing except the whole truth. I didn't wanna hear this shit, but that didn't make it any less authentic. The purpose for having good people around you was to catch the shit that was moving past you. I loved Mo-Mo because she didn't miss much, and neither did I, so we complemented each other perfectly.

"I hate you sometimes…but I love you more," I said, pulling her towards me and hugging her tightly.

"The feeling is definitely mutual."

"Awww, you two are sooo cute," Fatz cooed, walking up on us.

"I like you, my nigga, don't fuck that up," I warned.

I hate to interrupt, but I need to know where to direct my niggas to go," he said.

I took a step back from Mo while thinking about how to handle the next step in our plan. The need for privacy was paramount but being in foreign territory right now wasn't a good idea.

"Just have them come to my house because right now. Being on home base outweighs my need to sneak around," I said.

"I got you and once they're here, I'll have someone posted outside to guard the perimeter," Fatz said, already tapping away on his phone.

"Good idea, bae, but uh, I hope you don't think I'm staying here while you two have all the fun," Mo said.

"Mo, we've had this conversation once already, and you know how I feel about repeating myself. You're dead, and dead people don't ride around saying boo!" I said.

"I understand that I'm dead, but if you're ready to bring the fight to Campa, then what does it matter if he knows I'm alive?" she asked logically.

"We're not taking the fight to him right this minute, so until we do, you can sit your happy ass here—"

"Or I can sit my happy ass in the safety of your house that's about to be heavily guarded, right?" she asked, smiling at me.

I looked at Fatz because I knew I didn't have any type of argument that was gonna hold her here, and if I was being one hundred percent honest, I wanted my bitch by my side because there was no one I trusted more to watch my back right now.

"I don't know why both of you are looking at me, because I ain't never won an argument against Mo," Fatz said.

"It's settled then. Let's go," she said, leading the way upstairs.

I was shaking my head as I followed her, but deep down I knew that this was the right move to make, because it allowed me to completely focus without watching my back. I could tell by the bluish tint to the sky that we were only a couple hours away from daylight. It felt like today could be the day of reckoning that I'd long known was on the horizon between Campa and me. A part of me had known the moment after he'd shot and killed my best friend in the whole world, my soul wouldn't stop being restless until I'd settled the score. It was true that money made the world go around, and I'd made a lot of money with Campa, but some things were worth more than money. Tony was one of those things, and I was okay with that.

"My niggas will be here in a couple hours," Fatz said from behind me.

"Ok. In the meantime, we—"

My phone vibrating in my pocket paused my sentence. When I pulled it out, I finally saw the number I'd been expecting since earlier.

"Hello?" I answered neutrally.

"I just heard we lost someone, what the hell is going on?" Campa asked, feigning real concern.

"Yeah, we did, but I don't know what's going on. I'm trying to piece everything together now, but...I'm-I'm just so fucked up about it."

"I know, sweetheart, I know. It's never easy to lose someone close to you, and you've lost more than anyone ever should. I promise you, we will get to the bottom of this though!" he vowed passionately.

"Thank you, Jefe, I really appreciate you. I have to go make the identification, and then I'm going to check with our sources to see what I can find out. After that, I will call you and let you know what progress I've made."

"That's fine. I will do what I can on my end of course, but I have to leave town on business later this afternoon, so make sure you call me as soon as you're free," he said.

"I will."

I hung up and turned to motion Fatz to follow me inside.

"What took you two so long?" Mo asked, looking irritated with her hands on her hips, standing by the back door.

"Campa called," I replied, moving past her, and deactivating the alarm.

"What did he say?" she asked impatiently.

I ignored her question until we were inside with the door locked and the alarm back on, sitting around my kitchen table. I quickly relayed my conversation with Campa, making Mo hold all her questions until the end.

"That nigga is coldblooded for real," Mo said, more angry than hurt by the truth of her statement.

"I could've told you that, especially after the way he shot Tony for no fucking reason," I said softly.

"You know what he's doing, right?" Fatz asked, looking directly at me.

"Trying to pinpoint my location while establishing an alibi out of the way. That way he can do what he has to do, and still make sure my team is loyal to him by not suspecting him as the one who killed me," I replied matter of factly.

"That's exactly what he's doing," Fatz said, clearly impressed by my quick analysis.

"So, what's our move?" Mo asked.

"We play all offense, so there's no need for defense," I said.

"Give me your keys, so I can pull your truck into the garage where no one can see it and figure out we're here. While I'm doing that, you two can shut down all the lights in the upper part of the house and relocate to the basement so we can plan," Fatz said.

I dug my keys out of my pocket and handed them to him, before leading him to the back door so I could deactivate the alarm again. Once he was gone, Mo and I went about making it look like no one was home at Casa de Snow, but we waited upstairs for Fatz to pull in the garage, so we could help him unload the guns. With that done, we reconvened in the basement, and put our thoughts together on how to wage a war we could win.

"So, give me the layout of Campa's house, so I can picture it in my mind," Fatz said, laying his head in Mo's lap.

For a second, I got caught up in how at ease they were with each other that he could lay his head in her lap, and she instantly started to play with his dreadlocks. It reminded me of my relationship with Zion, and it made my heart ache.

"I, uh, I've actually got the layout of his house, or the model rather, because I was thinking about getting one like it," I replied, looking for the blueprints in my phone.

"Does Campa know you have these pictures?" Mo asked, looking over Fatz's shoulder when I passed him my phone.

"I doubt it, because it was a while ago when I was talking about doing that. Even if he did though, he wouldn't put it together with what's going on and think I'm about to come for that ass."

Both of them nodded their heads in agreement, and for a while we just sat around discussing possible penetration points for Campa's compound. It was about an hour and a half into this when Fatz's phone went off, and he let me know that his team was here. I took a seat on the couch beside Mo while he went to let his people in.

"Do you know any of the niggas he's brought out here?" I asked.

"I think I know a few because he said some names from when he was locked up, and if I'm right, then they're the type of niggas that we want involved."

"I hope you're right because there are a lot of moving parts to this situation. Campa is backed by some of the heaviest hitters, so even killing him is just the beginning, not the end," I said.

I looked her directly in the eyes to make sure she understood all she was signing up for, but I didn't see an ounce of fear.

"Even if you weren't my bitch, I'd still be in this until the end, because they tried to hit me and my nigga. Nobody comes for me and I don't come right back for them!"

The fire I saw in her eyes right now was part of what made me love her, and if I hadn't heard footsteps coming down the stairs, I might've been tempted to make her cum quick because I was turned on. Instead, I turned my attention to the niggas filing down the stairs behind Fatz, making sure to put my mind in the right place and put my face on resting bitch mode. When the last man reached the bottom of the steps, he fell into line next to the man in front of him, and they all stood silent, waiting.

"May I introduce some hittas that don't know how to quit?" Fatz said smiling.

I evaluated each man silently, making eye contact with each one to see who flinched or had signs of discomfort.

"What has Fatz told you about why you're here?" I asked.

"Let's take care of the introductions first, shall we?" Fatz said.

I gave him a look to let him know my patience was beyond thin, but Mo took my hand in hers and gave it a gentle squeeze.

"I know you, don't I?" Mo asked, pointing at a slim built brown-skinned nigga covered in tattoos, with long dreadlocks tied up in a ponytail.

"You do," he acknowledged.

"That's Red Gunz, my homie from Portsmouth, Virginia. A hitta cut from the cloth reserved for kings," Fatz said.

"Kings, huh?" I asked.

The smile Red Gunz gave me was one I'd seen before, but only on certain killers' faces. The type of nigga Gunz was, was one that asked no questions about why someone had to die, and who you wanted to send with them.

"The one next to him is J5," Mo said, pointing out a tall light-skinned nigga with a grit on his face that showed the golds in his mouth. I glanced at him briefly, taking in his six-foot, two-hundred-eighty pounds in one sweep, but my eyes came back to the gun in his shoulder holster.

"It's a 1911 .45, huh?" I asked.

"Custom made with the wood handle engraved," he replied.

"What does the handle say?" I asked.

"Southside."

"Ah, so I take it you're from Richmond, Virginia," I said.

His smile answered that question for me.

"Well, ain't no need to guess where I'm from, because it should be obvious."

This comment came from a short, stocky, brown-skinned nigga with a big beard and an arrogant smile. I looked at Mo, but she shook her head and looked at Fatz.

"Oh, y'all got jokes like you don't know a muthafucka from the shore?" the man asked.

"This is my nigga, Vontrell, from Eastern Shore," Fatz said laughing.

I noticed Vontrell had a quick smile and infectious laugh, but the eyes never lied about a killer's capabilities.

"What has Fatz told you about why you're here?" I asked again, crossing my legs slowly.

"A nigga needs his head knocked off…and those around him do too," Red Gunz replied.

"Indeed. We're gonna bring the fight to him though, so we're gonna give you the layout for the property we're running down on, and then we'll formulate a plan," I said.

"Do you mind if we bring our niggas inside, because sitting outside in their cars in this neighborhood is sure to attract attention," J5 said.

"That's fine. Fatz, get them set up upstairs, and put some niggas on the perimeter like we talked about," I replied.

Fatz nodded and led his dudes back upstairs. Once they were gone, I turned to Mo.

"Okay, so based on what you know, what do you think? I mean, are we war ready?" I asked.

"I think so. I mean, I know two of the three, and I doubt they would put niggas on their team that ain't like-minded. We're as ready as we can be right now."

I thought about what she said, as well as what she didn't say, and weighed that against my options. I hated to go at this thing half-cocked, but I damn sure wasn't about to let Campa box me in until I had no way out. That left me with only one option. We were going to war.

Aryanna

Chapter 20

"Hey little man, what are you up to?" I asked, smiling.

"Hi, Mom! I miss you!"

"I miss you too, baby, and I'll see you soon, don't worry."

"How soon?" he asked.

I didn't wanna lie to him, and it was for that reason I'd prepared him for this day long ago. When I'd devised this plan of escape to keep my son safe, I'd known that when he was old enough, I'd have to somewhat explain to him why he'd have to drop everything and run at a moment's notice one day. I worked hard to protect him, gave him everything he could possibly want and need, and spent as much time with him as possible. I did all of this because I knew the life I'd chosen when Zion died was one of borrowed time and stolen moments. There was no retirement plan for the real gangsters, and we very rarely got to see the smile of death, because he came from behind us. So, I had to make the best of the life I was given, and that meant doing everything possible to make sure my son got to live to a ripe old age. That meant I would kill and die for him over and over.

"You know I won't lie to you, Junior, so I really don't know when I'm gonna see you. You know you're safe though, right?"

"I know, Mom, and I know that this plan of yours is all just to protect me, but I'm older now and I—"

"Zion, I know you wanna protect me, but that's not your responsibility, son. I'm your mom and that'll never change so please, let's not fight about it," I said.

I could tell by the way he clenched his jaw and looked away from the iPad screen that he was frustrated, and I had no doubts that his frustration rested solely with me.

"I love you, Junior, and I hope you remember that no matter how mad you get at me."

"Don't say that, Mom," he replied quickly.

"Huh? Why not?" I asked, confused.

"Because-because it sounds like you're saying goodbye, and you told me we never say goodbye. You promised me!"

"Okay, sweetie, okay. Calm down. I wasn't trying to say goodbye to you, I just don't like when you're mad at me because it makes me think you don't know just how much I love you," I said.

For a second, he just stared at me, and I could feel how badly he wanted this not to be a FaceTime call, but an actual situation where he could reach out and touch me. It hurt my heart because I could tell my little man was aching for me, and the fact that I wasn't there, made me feel like a failure. I knew I had to handle this for his sake, but he didn't know and understand that. I refused to lie to him, but there was only so much truth I could trust him with at his age. He wasn't ignorant to how the world worked, I simply couldn't let him know how close the boogieman really was to his front door.

"I know you love me, Mom…and I know that anything you do for me is the right thing to do. I'm just bored and I miss you."

"Do you wanna go somewhere else?" I asked.

"No, I like it here in the mountains, and the snow is beautiful!"

"I told you that, didn't I? There's nothing like fresh snow, and since that's your last name, I thought it was time for you to actually experience it," I said.

The smile lighting up his face made my heart pound harder and faster in my chest, and I prayed that Zion Sr. was looking down over his son right now and smiling too.

"Make sure you take some pictures," I said.

"I will, but…"

"You wish Alexia was there with you or could see it too, huh?" I asked.

"How did you know, Mom?" he asked, looking surprised.

"I know because you're my son, and it's my job to know what's bothering you."

"Oh. Well yeah, that's what I was thinking. It's fun out here in Colorado, but I miss being home…I miss Alexia," he confessed, avoiding eye contact with me.

As usual, it made my heart hurt to hear my little man growing up when it came to the opposite sex, but now wasn't the time for me to consider my feelings.

"Would you feel better if Alexia was there with you?" I asked.

His face immediately lit up with a huge grin that made me smile, but just as swiftly his frown was back.

"Yeah, I would like her to be here, but I wouldn't want her to be away from her family. I know how much that hurts, and I don't want her to hurt like that," he said softly.

This time it was my turn to avoid his penetrating stare, and at the same time I was trying not to cry. The decisions that both me and his father had made had somewhat robbed our son of his innocence, and I hated that. He shouldn't have to know what it was like to miss his family, nor should the girl that he was in puppy love with, but it was now part reality.

"Junior, do you trust me?"

"Yes, Mommy, I trust you," he replied without hesitation.

"Then trust me when I tell you that one day, all of this will be a good memory, and in the meantime, I want you to just enjoy yourself. I'll see you soon, I promise, but until then I'll send you someone to keep you company."

"Who are you sending?" he asked, curiously.

"Don't worry, you'll see. You just be on your best behavior or I'ma kick your whole ass when you get home."

"Yes, ma'am. I love you, Mommy."

"I love you too, sweetheart, and I'll call you in the morning."

We blew each other kisses, and then I waited until his screen went blank before I put the iPad down and laid across my bed. I stared at the ceiling looking for answers that definitely weren't up there, while trying to organize my thoughts for what was to come. A soft knock on the door interrupted my thoughts, but it gave me a reason not to cry.

"Come in," I said.

Mo came in and closed the door behind her before moving to lay on the bed beside me.

"How's Junior doing?"

"He's alright, but I can tell he misses me bad. It breaks my fucking heart!" I replied, fighting the anger that was trying to take the place of my sadness.

"Did you tell him that Alexia was coming out there with him?"

"No, I just told him I was sending someone out there to keep him company," I said, smiling at the thought of his reaction to Alexia showing up.

"I know he's gonna be happy...and that probably kills you."

"Honestly, I'll just settle for my baby being happy right now, you know? I hate I'm having to put him through this shit, Mo!"

"I know, bae, I know. That's why we need to get this shit over with ASAP, so that we can bring little man home. My step-daughter too."

Hearing her refer to Alexia like this made me look over at her to gauge her frame of mind right now.

"Your step-daughter, huh? So, that would make Fatz your…"

"You know damn well what it makes Fatz, bitch, so stop acting slow before I slap you," she said, elbowing me in the side.

"Ow, bitch! Don't get mad at me for seeking clarification."

"Yeah, whatever…I mean, Fatz is a good nigga, and he's the only nigga I've dealt with that I know for sure loves me for more than just my beauty. I feel like even without the amazing sex, I'd still wanna be with him, and that's saying a lot."

"That is saying a lot, but I'm just glad you've found happiness," I said.

"You really mean that, Claudette?"

"Yeah, bitch! I don't want your ass dying alone, and I'm getting too old for you to keep trying to fold me up into a pretzel and eat this pussy!"

We both laughed hard at that, mainly because of the imagery and because we knew I wasn't built for all that flexible shit. We definitely got it poppin between them sheets, but I'd trade her happiness for that any day of the week.

"So, does he know he's in this until death?" I asked, taking her hand in mine.

"It was his idea. We'd had conversations about it when he was still inside, but you know them niggas will promise the pope that they can deliver Jesus for a shot of pussy. So far, he's kept his word about everything he's ever told me though, and while you were up here talking to Junior, he brought up forever again."

"Sounds like the nigga is serious…I like that. He could've shoplifted the pussy and head and been on his way, but he's staying around and risking his life in the process. Take it from someone who had everything in one man once upon a time and listen to me when I tell you, you better not let him go. Hold on to him tightly, and love him with every breath in your body," I said sincerely.

She squeezed my hand and I could feel her heart beating through her fingertips. I knew it was a sick form of irony to find love and have to put it to the test so early in by going into hell together and praying you both made it out alive. In a perfect world, neither of them would have to experience this, but Mo wouldn't let me go to war by myself, and Fatz wouldn't let Mo out of his sight. So, ride we would, and we would win.

"It's almost nightfall, so is everyone ready?" I asked.

"Yeah. Red Gunz took his people and went to set up not far from Campa's house, so he could watch the traffic in and out. Once we're inside, Vontrell and J5 will cover the east and west sides of the property, working their way in while making sure that nobody gets out alive."

"Are you sure it's wise for you to go with us?" I asked, looking over at her.

"I'm not leaving my man's side or yours, so don't ask or suggest it again, unless you're trying to fight a bitch."

I smiled widely because that was the exact answer I expected from her crazy ass. A knock at the door made me sit up and pull her along with me.

"Yeah?"

Fatz stuck his head in the doorway.

"Everyone is in place, it's all on you now," he said.

I nodded before pulling my phone out the pocket of my black cargo pants. I dialed Campa's number and waited patiently for him to answer.

"Hola, Jefa. How are you holding up?" he asked.

"I've been better, but you know like I do, death is only a part of life."

"True indeed, true indeed. It is the most beautiful part of life if you ask me, and that's why I know when it's my time to go, I will greet death with a big grin," he replied.

"Will you? Well, I hope that's not too soon, Jefe, because I need your help to seek vengeance for those I've lost," I said.

"You know I will help you in any way I can, Claudette, all you needed to do was ask."

"I know, Jefe, but I just don't want to discuss these matters over the phone. Are you somewhere we can meet, or have you already left town to handle your business?" I asked calmly.

"I told you I wouldn't leave until I heard from you, and you know that I'm nothing, if not a man of my word. I'm actually at home tying up some loose ends of my own, but you're more than welcome to come over. You might even enjoy the festivities I'm putting together."

Something about the way he made this statement gave me a funny feeling in the pit of my stomach, but I knew there was absolutely no turning back now.

"I'll be there shortly," I replied.

"I'll be waiting."

Once I hung up the phone, I looked at Mo first and then Fatz before I replayed the part of the conversation they couldn't hear.

"Does it sound like he has any idea about what's coming?" Fatz asked.

"No, but he's definitely up to something of his own," I replied.

"That's good, because that means he's preoccupied," Mo said.

Her words rang true, but there was still that feeling in the pit of my stomach, gnawing at me in a way I couldn't ignore.

"What do you wanna do, Snow?" Fatz asked, after I'd gone completely still for a moment.

193

As crazy as it sounded, I was trying with all my might to channel Zion, but I wasn't getting anything. That meant that all I had to go on were my own instincts, and they would have to be enough.

"Load up and let's ride," I said.

We all went downstairs and grabbed everything that we would need for the upcoming confrontation. The plan was simply that me, Fatz, and Mo were gonna go in the house and lay shit down. Once the shooting started, everyone would descend on the compound like a swarm of angry insects. After that, it was in God's hands...or the devil's. We strapped up, put the extra guns in my truck, and got on the move. We met up with Red Gunz about two miles from Campa's compound to get an update on everything.

"How does shit look?" I asked.

"It was quiet until about fifteen minutes ago, and then a five-truck caravan came through. I couldn't see how many people were in the back of each truck, but it's safe to say you're outnumbered going in."

I looked at Fatz and Mo, but neither of them showed any signs of wanting to change the plans we'd made.

"Sounds like good odds for us," I said, rolling up the window and pulling off in the direction of Campa's house.

We rode the rest of the way in silence, and when I pulled up out front, none of us wasted a moment getting out of the truck. It was go-time.

Chapter 21

"Stay close and move fast, because I doubt it takes him long to realize his surveillance has been signal jammed," I said, leading the way up to his front door.

I knew the code to get in the door without having a key, so I quickly entered it and we stepped inside. I could immediately hear voices, but I couldn't pinpoint their exact location and that left me feeling disoriented.

"Who are you?" a short, stocky Spanish man asked.

"Me? Oh, I'm a friend of El Jefe," I said.

"Jefe is busy, so—"

Whatever he was gonna say got stuck in his throat, because Mo had her gun pressed up against his mustache. In rapid Spanish, she told him to lay down on the ground. When he didn't move, she cocked back her hand and smacked him with her pistol.

"Maybe he just didn't understand your Spanish," I said.

"He does now," she replied, smiling sweetly.

I stepped over his body and continued on in the direction that I heard the voices coming from. When I pinpointed Campa's office as the location the voices were coming from, I pulled my gun out, and signaled for Fatz to let everybody know we were seconds from getting this shit popping. Given the amount of SUV's Red Gunz had seen, I was expecting to run into a lot of resistance in these hallways, but surprisingly, we made it to Campa's office without having to fire a shot or render anyone else unconscious.

"Fatz, post up, and shoot anyone not with us. Mo, come with me and stay alert," I whispered.

They both nodded their understanding and we moved. I took a deep breath and led the way around the corner fast with my gun up and ready.

"It took you long enough to get here, Jefa," Campa said, smiling widely even with my gun pointed at him.

I did a quick head count, and from what I could see, there were six big men around Campa. I wasn't worried though, because I had enough bullets for everybody.

"Sorry to keep you waiting, Jefe, but don't worry, I'll make it up to you right now," I said, squeezing the trigger just a little tighter.

"Before you do, you might wanna hear what she has to say," Campa said, still smiling.

I glanced over at Mo briefly, but the look of confusion on her face matched mine. I opened my mouth to ask him what the fuck he was talking about, but the answer quickly revealed itself. Two big men stepped back, and Phillisa stepped forward.

"Wh-what the fuck are you doing here?" I asked.

I could hear the shakiness in my own voice, but I was helpless to change it.

"I can explain, Claudette," Phillisa said.

"Oh, this should be interesting," Campa said, clapping his hands excitedly.

"There's no need to explain, I told you I had this under control," I said.

"By this, you mean coming here to kill me, right? The one who's looked out for you?" Campa asked.

"Looked out for me? Ain't you the same nigga trying to kill me right now?" I asked, looking at him like he was crazy.

"I have my reasons for everything I do," he replied defensively.

"Oh, like killing Zion?" Phillisa said angrily.

"Wh-what the fuck are you talking about Phillisa? Campa didn't kill Zion. I know that because I killed the men responsible for Zion's death," I said.

"You killed who Campa told you to kill, but he was lying," she replied insistently.

"You don't know what the fuck you're talking about, Phillisa, because you weren't here, so just—"

"But I was here, Claudette," she said softly.

I knew damn well I wasn't tripping because I remembered exactly who was in the room when I dropped the hammer on somebody for the first time. I knew Campa knew too, because he'd been there, but when I looked at him to reaffirm what I was saying he had a weird look on his face.

"Campa, what the hell is she babbling about? And don't say you don't know, because I know she's your daughter," I said.

"Correction, she was my daughter, but she fucked that up."

"By falling in love, Papa? How? Love shouldn't have made you disown me or kill the man I loved!" she replied heatedly, spinning around to face Campa.

"Zion had no goddamn business loving you back, and I warned him to stay away from you!"

"But, Papa—"

"Wait…hold up a motherfucking minute…are-are you trying to say my husband had something going on with your daughter?" I asked slowly.

The heat that flashed in Campa's eyes said it all, but the look of guilt Phillisa turned around and faced me with knocked the wind out of me and made me drop my gun.

"You-you-you and my-my Zion—"

"Claudette, I can explain—"

"Explain it to God, bitch, because I never liked you anyway," Mo said, levelling her gun at Phillisa.

Before I could utter another word, the night came alive with bullets.

To Be Continued...
A Dope Boy's Queen 2
Coming Soon

Submission Guideline

Submit the first three chapters of your completed manuscript to ldpsubmissions@gmail.com, subject line: Your book's title. The manuscript must be in a .doc file and sent as an attachment. Document should be in Times New Roman, double spaced and in size 12 font. Also, provide your synopsis and full contact information. If sending multiple submissions, they must each be in a separate email.

Have a story but no way to send it electronically? You can still submit to LDP/Ca$h Presents. Send in the first three chapters, written or typed, of your completed manuscript to:

LDP: Submissions Dept
Po Box 944
Stockbridge, Ga 30281

DO NOT send original manuscript. Must be a duplicate.

Provide your synopsis and a cover letter containing your full contact information.

Thanks for considering LDP and Ca$h Presents.

Coming Soon from Lock Down Publications/Ca$h Presents

BOW DOWN TO MY GANGSTA

By **Ca$h**

TORN BETWEEN TWO

By **Coffee**

THE STREETS STAINED MY SOUL **II**

By **Marcellus Allen**

BLOOD OF A BOSS **VI**

SHADOWS OF THE GAME II

By **Askari**

LOYAL TO THE GAME **IV**

By **T.J. & Jelissa**

A DOPEBOY'S PRAYER **II**

By **Eddie "Wolf" Lee**

IF LOVING YOU IS WRONG… **III**

By **Jelissa**

TRUE SAVAGE **VII**

MIDNIGHT CARTEL III

DOPE BOY MAGIC IV

By **Chris Green**

BLAST FOR ME **III**

A SAVAGE DOPEBOY III

CUTTHROAT MAFIA II

By **Ghost**

A HUSTLER'S DECEIT III

KILL ZONE **II**

BAE BELONGS TO ME III

A DOPE BOY'S QUEEN II

By **Aryanna**

CHAINED TO THE STREETS III

By **J-Blunt**

KING OF NEW YORK V

COKE KINGS IV

BORN HEARTLESS IV

By **T.J. Edwards**

GORILLAZ IN THE BAY V

TEARS OF A GANGSTA II

De'Kari

THE STREETS ARE CALLING II

Duquie Wilson

KINGPIN KILLAZ IV

STREET KINGS III

PAID IN BLOOD III

CARTEL KILLAZ IV

DOPE GODS II

Hood Rich

SINS OF A HUSTLA II

ASAD

TRIGGADALE III

Elijah R. Freeman

KINGZ OF THE GAME V

Playa Ray

SLAUGHTER GANG IV

RUTHLESS HEART IV
By Willie Slaughter
THE HEART OF A SAVAGE III
By Jibril Williams
FUK SHYT II
By Blakk Diamond
THE DOPEMAN'S BODYGAURD II
By Tranay Adams
TRAP GOD II
By Troublesome
YAYO III
A SHOOTER'S AMBITION III
By S. Allen
GHOST MOB
Stilloan Robinson
KINGPIN DREAMS II
By Paper Boi Rari
CREAM
By Yolanda Moore
SON OF A DOPE FIEND II
By Renta
FOREVER GANGSTA II
GLOCKS ON SATIN SHEETS II
By Adrian Dulan
LOYALTY AIN'T PROMISED II
By Keith Williams
THE PRICE YOU PAY FOR LOVE II

DOPE GIRL MAGIC II

By Destiny Skai

TOE TAGZ III

By Ah'Million

CONFESSIONS OF A GANGSTA II

By Nicholas Lock

PAID IN KARMA III

By **Meesha**

I'M NOTHING WITHOUT HIS LOVE II

By Monet Dragun

CAUGHT UP IN THE LIFE II

By Robert Baptiste

NEW TO THE GAME III

By **Malik D. Rice**

LIFE OF A SAVAGE III

By **Romell Tukes**

QUIET MONEY II

By **Trai'Quan**

THE STREETS MADE ME II

By **Larry D. Wright**

THE ULTIMATE SACRIFICE VI

By **Anthony Fields**

THE LIFE OF A HOOD STAR

By Ca$h & Rashia Wilson

<u>Available Now</u>

RESTRAINING ORDER **I & II**

By **CA$H & Coffee**

LOVE KNOWS NO BOUNDARIES **I II & III**

By **Coffee**

RAISED AS A GOON I, II, III & IV

BRED BY THE SLUMS I, II, III

BLAST FOR ME I & II

ROTTEN TO THE CORE I II III

A BRONX TALE I, II, III

DUFFEL BAG CARTEL I II III IV

HEARTLESS GOON I II III IV

A SAVAGE DOPEBOY I II

HEARTLESS GOON I II III

DRUG LORDS I II III

CUTTHROAT MAFIA

By **Ghost**

LAY IT DOWN **I & II**

LAST OF A DYING BREED

BLOOD STAINS OF A SHOTTA I & II III

By **Jamaica**

LOYAL TO THE GAME I II III

LIFE OF SIN I, II III

By **TJ & Jelissa**

BLOODY COMMAS I & II

SKI MASK CARTEL I II & III

KING OF NEW YORK I II,III IV

RISE TO POWER I II III

COKE KINGS I II III

BORN HEARTLESS I II III

By **T.J. Edwards**

IF LOVING HIM IS WRONG…I & II

LOVE ME EVEN WHEN IT HURTS I II III

By **Jelissa**

WHEN THE STREETS CLAP BACK I & II III

THE HEART OF A SAVAGE I II

By **Jibril Williams**

A DISTINGUISHED THUG STOLE MY HEART I II & III

LOVE SHOULDN'T HURT I II III IV

RENEGADE BOYS I II III IV

PAID IN KARMA I II

By **Meesha**

A GANGSTER'S CODE I &, II III

A GANGSTER'S SYN I II III

THE SAVAGE LIFE I II III

CHAINED TO THE STREETS I II

By J-Blunt

PUSH IT TO THE LIMIT

By **Bre' Hayes**

BLOOD OF A BOSS **I, II, III, IV, V**

SHADOWS OF THE GAME

By **Askari**

THE STREETS BLEED MURDER **I, II & III**

Aryanna

THE HEART OF A GANGSTA I II& III

By **Jerry Jackson**

CUM FOR ME I II III IV V

An **LDP Erotica Collaboration**

BRIDE OF A HUSTLA **I II & II**

THE FETTI GIRLS **I, II& III**

CORRUPTED BY A GANGSTA I, II III, IV

BLINDED BY HIS LOVE

THE PRICE YOU PAY FOR LOVE

DOPE GIRL MAGIC

By **Destiny Skai**

WHEN A GOOD GIRL GOES BAD

By **Adrienne**

THE COST OF LOYALTY I II III

By Kweli

A GANGSTER'S REVENGE **I II III & IV**

THE BOSS MAN'S DAUGHTERS I II III IV V

A SAVAGE LOVE **I & II**

BAE BELONGS TO ME I II

A HUSTLER'S DECEIT I, II, III

WHAT BAD BITCHES DO I, II, III

SOUL OF A MONSTER I II III

KILL ZONE

A DOPE BOY'S QUEEN

By **Aryanna**

A KINGPIN'S AMBITON

A KINGPIN'S AMBITION **II**

206

I MURDER FOR THE DOUGH

By **Ambitious**

TRUE SAVAGE I II III IV V VI

DOPE BOY MAGIC I, II, III

MIDNIGHT CARTEL I II

By **Chris Green**

A DOPEBOY'S PRAYER

By **Eddie "Wolf" Lee**

THE KING CARTEL **I, II & III**

By **Frank Gresham**

THESE NIGGAS AIN'T LOYAL **I, II & III**

By **Nikki Tee**

GANGSTA SHYT **I II &III**

By **CATO**

THE ULTIMATE BETRAYAL

By **Phoenix**

BOSS'N UP **I , II & III**

By **Royal Nicole**

I LOVE YOU TO DEATH

By Destiny J

I RIDE FOR MY HITTA

I STILL RIDE FOR MY HITTA

By **Misty Holt**

LOVE & CHASIN' PAPER

By **Qay Crockett**

TO DIE IN VAIN

SINS OF A HUSTLA

By **ASAD**

BROOKLYN HUSTLAZ

By **Boogsy Morina**

BROOKLYN ON LOCK I & II

By **Sonovia**

GANGSTA CITY

By **Teddy Duke**

A DRUG KING AND HIS DIAMOND I & II III

A DOPEMAN'S RICHES

HER MAN, MINE'S TOO I, II

CASH MONEY HO'S

By Nicole Goosby

TRAPHOUSE KING **I II & III**

KINGPIN KILLAZ I II III

STREET KINGS I II

PAID IN BLOOD **I II**

CARTEL KILLAZ I II III

DOPE GODS

By **Hood Rich**

LIPSTICK KILLAH **I, II, III**

CRIME OF PASSION I II & III

By **Mimi**

STEADY MOBBN' **I, II, III**

THE STREETS STAINED MY SOUL

By **Marcellus Allen**

WHO SHOT YA **I, II, III**

SON OF A DOPE FIEND

A Dope Boy's Queen

Renta
GORILLAZ IN THE BAY **I II III IV**
TEARS OF A GANGSTA
DE'KARI
TRIGGADALE I II
Elijah R. Freeman
GOD BLESS THE TRAPPERS I, II, III
THESE SCANDALOUS STREETS I, II, III
FEAR MY GANGSTA I, II, III
THESE STREETS DON'T LOVE NOBODY I, II
BURY ME A G I, II, III, IV, V
A GANGSTA'S EMPIRE I, II, III, IV
THE DOPEMAN'S BODYGAURD
Tranay Adams
THE STREETS ARE CALLING
Duquie Wilson
MARRIED TO A BOSS... I II III
By Destiny Skai & Chris Green
KINGZ OF THE GAME I II III IV
Playa Ray
SLAUGHTER GANG I II III
RUTHLESS HEART I II III
By Willie Slaughter
FUK SHYT
By Blakk Diamond
DON'T F#CK WITH MY HEART I II
By Linnea

209

Aryanna

ADDICTED TO THE DRAMA I II III

By Jamila

YAYO I II

A SHOOTER'S AMBITION I II

By S. Allen

TRAP GOD

By Troublesome

FOREVER GANGSTA

GLOCKS ON SATIN SHEETS

By Adrian Dulan

TOE TAGZ I II

By Ah'Million

KINGPIN DREAMS

By Paper Boi Rari

CONFESSIONS OF A GANGSTA

By Nicholas Lock

I'M NOTHING WITHOUT HIS LOVE

By Monet Dragun

CAUGHT UP IN THE LIFE

By Robert Baptiste

NEW TO THE GAME I II

By **Malik D. Rice**

Life of a Savage I II

By **Romell Tukes**

LOYALTY AIN'T PROMISED

By Keith Williams

Quiet Money

By **Trai'Quan**
THE STREETS MADE ME
By **Larry D. Wright**
THE ULTIMATE SACRIFICE I, II, III, IV, V
By **Anthony Fields**
THE LIFE OF A HOOD STAR
By **Ca$h & Rashia Wilson**

BOOKS BY LDP'S CEO, CA$H

TRUST IN NO MAN

TRUST IN NO MAN 2

TRUST IN NO MAN 3

BONDED BY BLOOD

SHORTY GOT A THUG

THUGS CRY

THUGS CRY 2

THUGS CRY 3

TRUST NO BITCH

TRUST NO BITCH 2

TRUST NO BITCH 3

TIL MY CASKET DROPS

RESTRAINING ORDER

RESTRAINING ORDER 2

IN LOVE WITH A CONVICT

LIFE OF A HOOD STAR

Coming Soon

BONDED BY BLOOD 2

BOW DOWN TO MY GANGSTA